AVALANCHE

A JACKLYN STONE THRILLER

JACKLYN STONE THRILLERS
BOOK 3

SUSAN SPECHT ORAM

Published by SOS Communications LLC in 2025

www.susanspechtoram.com

First Edition

ISBN (paperback): 979-8-9926053-7-2

ISBN (e-book): 979-8-9926053-6-5

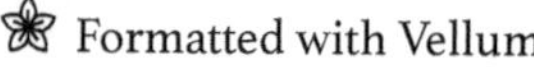 Formatted with Vellum

PREVIOUSLY

PREVIOUSLY IN:

SHORE LODGE

Jacklyn Stone, a grieving widow and garden store owner, is admitted by her greedy son to a secure psychiatric facility. She must escape to rescue her dog and reclaim her home.

BY MIDNIGHT

Jacklyn helps friends gather money to keep a debt collector at bay, but the clock is ticking in a race against time.

THE WINTER STORM

Jacklyn gathers friends and returns to Shore Lodge to free four residents from a secure psychiatric unit. But a storm is brewing and her son is out to thwart her every move.

THE COLD NIGHT

A missing teenage girl. A frantic mother. A snowstorm traps Jacklyn with her devious son.

1

DUSTY

Heading to my new hometown near the mountains, I frown. Two nights ago, I was trapped with my mother in a storm. When the roads opened up, I shoved sandwiches in my coat pockets and left her house. She might think our struggle is over, but I'm not done fighting to get my company back. This is just a lull in our storm.

Taking a drag of my cigarette, I blow out smoke and blink at a yard sale sign. I'm bored, so I'll stop and take a look. Maybe I'll find something to thwart my mom's plans. I shrug, because it's unlikely, and pull over and park near Foothills, Washington, population eight-hundred.

A mountain looms over town, and I nod to it. Grinding my cigarette butt under my boot heel, I wander past tables set up on a lawn. My eyes flit over worn leather shoes, a dusty CD player and neck ties with food stains.

A ruddy cheeked man about my size, over six feet tall, stands behind a card table. He says, "Need anything? I'll make you a deal. I'm about to close up for the day. Forecast says it's going to rain really hard."

I glance up at dark gray clouds hovering overhead. A pair of snowshoes grabs my attention, and I pick them up, examining the wood frames. They look solid and like they could hold my weight. I'd like to venture out in the mountains, explore the winter landscape and write poems in the new fallen, fresh snow.

Biting my lip, I come up with a plan. First, I'll find ways to foul my mother's construction project, and then I'll take a well-deserved break by heading out into the wilderness, all by myself.

Pointing at the snowshoes, I ask, "How much for these?"

He shoves his hands in his jeans packets and rocks back. "Those are old, but they still work. How about ten bucks? Got to clear this stuff out from my dad's place."

I glance at weeds growing in front of a rundown rambler and wait a beat, figuring he's desperate, and I'll get a lower price. I don't need snowshoes, and I'm broke, but this will be my reward for battling with Mom and working behind her back. I bet he'll mark the price down if I pretend to care, so I say, "Your dad okay?"

Shaking his head, he looks down at the ground. "Sadly, he passed away."

"Sorry to hear that. Must be rough."

He wipes a tear from his eye. "Sure is. Tell you what, why don't you just take them? Everything here reminds me of Dad. It's too painful to be around all of this."

"Wow, that's generous, but I wouldn't want to take advantage of you."

He opens his arms and gestures to the tables. In a tight voice, he says, "Take anything you want. Be my guest."

I pick up the snowshoes and a motor cycle helmet, which will come in handy if I barge into Mom's house to terrorize her one night. "I'll take these, if it's all right."

"Sure thing, but be careful if you use those snowshoes. The weather forecast called for warming. Whatever you do, don't go out in the mountains now. We have avalanche warnings. Wait a week and don't go alone."

"Thanks, man, I appreciate it. Hang in there."

He clears his throat. "So long. Take care of those for my dad."

He turns away, wiping his eyes. I walk to my truck and rain starts to drizzle down. Driving away, I head to the musty, damp cabin I recently rented.

Turning up a rutted dirt road, I clench my jaw. I know the old guy is probably right, but I'll snowshoe in the mountains whenever I want. I'll probably go alone, because no one seems to want to be around me, given gossip about how I admitted Mom to the psychiatric unit at Shore Lodge.

I sigh and say to myself, "I'm fine on my own. I don't need anyone."

2

JACKLYN

A chain saw whines and saw dust flies as workers in yellow safety vests cut up a tree that fell in my front yard during a recent storm. I wipe my brow and pick up branches on the ground, tossed down by a recent winter storm. Sniffing the air, briny sea air wafting off from the channel brings a smile to my face.

The chipper whirs, and I toss leaves into a yard waste bin. I'm coming up on a year since my husband Albert suddenly died on our wedding anniversary, and I found a way to survive, despite my son's best efforts to lock me away forever in Shore Lodge. A movement catches my eye, and I turn to see five raccoons walking past. One stops and stares at me, as if miffed I'm not giving handouts like my new neighbor next door does twice a day.

The chipper grinds to a halt, and in the sudden silence, I hear a chittering sound coming from a tree.

Craning my neck, I meet the gaze of a raccoon perched on a branch maybe eight feet up, looking down at me.

A chill runs up my spine, and I shake it off.

My friend Mercury comes over, pulling off his work gloves. "They're almost done. Anything else you want them to trim or chop down while they're here?"

I arch an eyebrow. "You know me better than to ask that. I'd like to keep every tree and plant where they are, come rain, come wind, come high water."

He chuckles. "I guessed as much but thought I'd ask."

I gesture to our wildlife audience. "Those cute bandits are starting to get on my nerves. I feel like they're watching my every move and more and more of them are coming. It reminds me of Hitchcock's movie, *The Birds*."

He tugs on his gray mustache. "Yeah, that was a creepy one."

I take his arm, and we head toward the house. "I'm ready to put my feet up. But I wonder what Dusty is up to." I frown as I go in the back door, but my dog bounds up to me, wiping away my worries.

He tugs on his gray mustache. "Probably plotting his revenge and holed up in the cabin he rented."

"Fine with me if he stays right there and doesn't show up in Millersville for many months to come."

Mercury laughs. "I wish, but it doesn't seem like he's the type to give up. I bet he'll be back."

I groan. "I know, and I'll be ready when that happens. I don't want my nemesis on the premises, strong-arming me and using intimidation to get what he wants. What a disaster Christmas Eve was."

He cocks his head and smiles. "It was dramatic, and I'm glad I got to watch it unfold first-hand. I don't doubt Dusty will be coming after you to get his company back, but I know you're more than able to stand up to him."

My stomach churns at the thought of a show down with my son. My beagle-mix dog trots over, nuzzling my hand. I bend and pet his soft ears, whispering, "You're the best dog in the world."

Mercury goes over to the coffee maker. "Cup of coffee?"

"Yes, thanks, and I need to get ahead of what Dusty might be cooking up for me to thwart my plans. I've got to head to City Hall to straighten out the mess with the new requirement for an environmental survey."

Washing my hands at the kitchen sink, I glance at patches of melting snow in the back yard. What a travesty it was when my husband died, and my son's greedy side was revealed. "I don't think Dusty will ever stop expecting me to give him all my money. He was going to sell this house out from under me."

Mercury pushes a button to start coffee brewing. "But you swam to shore and stopped him. You can do it again, if you have to."

I blow out a breath and sink into a kitchen chair. "I wish he'd stop pestering me for handouts. But I'm probably a fool if I don't expect the same thing to happen again. I'd better buckle up and make a plan to fend him off."

Mercury leans against the kitchen counter, crossing his arms and chuckling. "You could make a protest sign that says, Keep your hands off my money. That means you, Dusty, my dear son."

I tip my head back and laugh. It feels good to let off steam and be light-hearted, but I know another show-down is on the horizon. My son doesn't give up when he wants something. He wants to take over my construction company and dig his calloused fingers into my bank accounts, taking and taking until there's no money left.

3

KELLY

I shove a gray hoodie and a black knit cap in my backpack and sling it over my shoulder. Heading to the door, I call, "Bye, Mom."

Mom runs into the living room, her hands wet from washing dishes. Her cheeks are flushed, and her cheeks are wet with tears. She's been crying a lot since I was brought home after my grandfather abducted me. "Where are you going? I thought we were going to hang out and drink hot chocolate by the fire?"

I shrug and look away before I cave. I've got to get away from her suffocating worry. She's been blaming herself for Granddad taking me, but it's not really her fault. I just can't tell her that or talk about it. I need to get out of this house and be on my own.

"I'm going to Plum's house, and I might stay over."

Mom comes over, eyes brimming with tears, and

wraps me in a warm hug that I'd normally melt into. I sigh and breathe in the smell of her sea-scented hair that comes from working on the water in her rescue boat.

I pull away and frown. "Being here reminds me of Granddad and how he forced me at knife point to get in his car. I have to get away."

She rests her hands on my shoulders. "Stay home instead. I'm making meatballs, and we'll hang out. We can watch a silly movie and eat popcorn." She cracks a smile.

Shaking my head, I feel horrible for pushing her away, but I can't stay in the house where I sat on the couch laughing with my grandfather. What a joke that was. I believed he was nice, before I saw his mean side that Mom warned me about.

I stare at the floor. "I just want to forget about it and go somewhere else for a while."

Mom's phone rings, and she glances at it. "I've got to take this, but don't leave. We need to talk."

"I'm sorry, Mom, I've got to go."

I wave goodbye and slip out of the house before she can stop me.

4

IRENA

I wave goodbye to Kelly, but she doesn't glance back, loping away with a long-legged stride. I swallow a lump in my throat and turn my attention to the phone call.

A woman says in a firm voice, "I'm calling from Newton Hospital in Centralia. Is this Irena Pickle?"

"That was my maiden name. Is this about my father?"

"I'm sorry to say he had another heart attack. He ripped out his IV and tried to leave the hospital against medical advice. When a security guard stopped him, your father collapsed. We managed to revive him, and he's in intensive care, if you'd like to visit him."

I shake my head. "You should handcuff him to the bed, because he'll try to escape again. He won't want to go back to prison. To tell you the truth, I don't really care what happens to him. He's not a good man."

"I understand, but we need a contact person, and he gave your name and number. Can I contact you again if his condition changes?"

"I wish you wouldn't. I hope he's in handcuffs, given what he did."

"Authorities have arrived and already handcuffed him. When he's in stable condition, he'll be transferred to the Federal Detention Facility prison in SeaTac south of Seattle."

I scowl. When he took Kelly, I was frantic and out of my mind with worry. Now that she's home, it's like a switch turned off inside her. Because of my horrible father, I lost my lovely thirteen-year-old girl, and in her place is an angry adolescent with a chip on her shoulder.

She says, "Is there someone else I should contact if there is a change in his condition?"

My friend's dog, Happy, sits staring at me and panting. I need to feed him soon. I blow out a breath. "There isn't anyone else. It's just me, so keep my name as his contact person."

"I'm sorry to hear what happened to your daughter."

My throat is tight with tears. "It's been tough on her, but she's safe at home. She's one of the lucky ones who got away."

We say goodbye and hang up. My phone dings with a text, and Tex, my new silent business partner, says she wants to meet to draw up a business plan. I've been avoiding doing that because I'd rather be out on the water, rescuing boaters in distress, but it's time we met and tackled this project. I text her, 'Come to my place in Millersville tomorrow at noon.'

She replies, 'Better if you come to the island. Bring Kelly with you.'

I study the ceiling and hesitate before answering. In the past, my daughter came along on boat trips when I worked or took friends out, and she had a good time. But I'm not sure how Kelly will feel about that now. I'll need to be firm and insist she come with me tomorrow to meet with Tex.

I reply, 'We'll be there.'

5

ABBY

I open my eyes and blink at a bright overhead light. A headache throbs, my right arm and leg ache and a brace is wrapped around my neck. Jack, my first crush and new husband, squeezes my hand, and I sigh.

He says, "You're back among the living. I was worried I lost you."

I say in a hoarse voice, "I'm not going away. You're stuck with me, Mr. Funny Fishbone."

He smiles, and lines around his eyes crinkle. "What happened?"

Wincing in pain, I squirm in bed. "I was heading down the freeway to see if Kelly was at a convenience store in Lancer. But the car ahead of me stopped all of a sudden, and I hit my brakes. My car kept going, skidding on snow and ice. Then I blacked out."

He fixes his brown-eyes on me. "I wish this hadn't happened. I thought when I got out of the hospital, we left our troubles behind."

"Kind of a role reversal, with me being the one in a hospital bed."

His Adam's apple bobs up and down. "I'm sorry, but I have to tell you something. The couple in the other car didn't make it. The police are considering charging you with vehicular homicide. They said you were driving too fast, considering the conditions, and they want to talk to you. They're waiting out in the hall."

I gasp. "Those poor people. But I wasn't driving too fast. I was going with the flow of traffic and below the speed limit. Tell them that."

He stands, clears his throat and takes his hand from mine. "You'd better tell them yourself, because here they are."

"Wait, did they find Kelly? Was she at that store? Did her grandfather take her?"

He pats my hand. "Kelly's fine, and they found her. That's all you need to know for now. Focus on getting better."

I say in a soft voice, "This isn't how our marriage was supposed to start."

A police officer in blue comes over, hitching up her pants and looking me over. "I'm Officer Nelson, and I have some questions about what happened before your accident."

My pulse quickens, and my armpits prick with sweat. I was trying to get to Kelly and help her. How did I end up in a hospital bed being questioned by the police?

6

____

KELLY

I head over to my friend Plum's house, but on the way, I notice two girls from my class at school hanging out on a street corner. They glance at me and go back to talking to each other. Drawn to them, I slow my steps .

"Hey, Kelly," Avery says. She's wearing heavy black eye liner and a black hoodie.

I stop and give them a faltering smile. "Hi."

"Heard you got kidnapped," Vista says, tugging on a strand of long blond hair streaked with green.

A lump forms in my throat. "Yeah."

Avery tilts her head. "Your grandfather did it?"

I shove my hands in my pockets. "Yeah."

"But you got away?"

I look down, shuffling my cut feet that were injured in the ordeal. "I did."

Vista stares. "How did you do it?"

I take a deep breath and say, "I broke a store window and used a snow shovel and a whip to keep him away. Luckily, state troopers and the FBI arrived and took me home."

They study me, mouths hanging open. Avery says, "That's cool."

I shrug. "See you around."

Vista smiles. "Why don't you hang out with us?"

"I've got to go meet Plum. Maybe another time."

I walk away and head to my best friend's house, but part of me wants to stay. Those two are known for being a little wild. I feel different from other kids, and I suspect Vista and Avery, as outsiders, would understand. I might want to change things up and join them.

7

___

IRENA

I text Kelly asking her to come home before bedtime because I made plans for us tomorrow. Tapping a toe, I wait to hear from her. Ten minutes later, my phone dings with a text from Kelly. 'Staying at Plum's. See you tomorrow.'

I frown and type back, fingers flying. 'That won't work. We're meeting Tex tomorrow on Grand Island, leaving at 10:30 in the morning. Come home.'

She replies, 'Go without me.'

I swallow a lump of frustration and call her, but she doesn't pick up, so I text, 'We'll have a fun time, like we used to.'

After a beat, she replies, 'The old me is gone. Everything's changed. Get used to it.'

I groan and shove my phone in my pocket. My docile

daughter has disappeared. I'll talk to her in person and sort this out.

Grabbing my car keys, I lock the house and head to Plum's house, which is five minutes away. I pull up and park outside a blue bungalow with white trim and stride through drizzling rain to the front door. Knocking hard with my knuckles, I tell myself to calm down. Breathe. It won't help my relationship with Kelly if I'm tense and upset.

No one comes to the door, so I knock again and give the doorbell a good push two times. The door opens, and Plum appears with my daughter behind her. I stare at Kelly and say, "I need to speak to Kelly for a few minutes. Okay if I come inside?"

Plum opens the door wide. "Sure."

Before I can step inside, Kelly charges out to the front porch, standing in the rain. She crosses her arms and says to Plum, 'I'll be back inside in a minute."

Kelly pulls the door closed, and we stand facing each other. Cold rain falls, dripping down the back of my neck.

She hisses. "Mom, what're you doing here? I said I'd be home tomorrow."

"You don't get to call the shots. I'm your mother, and I do. We're going to Grand Island tomorrow morning, whether you like it or not."

She blinks back tears. "What about what I want? When do I get to have a choice? I should have a say in everything I do from now on. I don't want to go, and that's final."

Adrenaline surges through me, and my hands clench. I want to reach out and shake her by the shoulders, but instead, I say in a slow, steady voice, "Get your things. We're going home."

Her jaw drops. "No way. We're baking a gluten-free pizza for dinner. It's in the oven. I can't leave now."

I open the door and stride inside, possessed by a demon-mother outrage and a driving need to seize control of the situation. Kelly has changed after the horrible kidnapping, and I don't know my daughter anymore. But I don't recognize myself and my new rage either.

Glancing around the living room, where art supplies are strewn on the couch and floor, I spot Kelly's backpack and sling it over my arm.

She follows me inside. "Mom, put that down. I'm staying here tonight."

Taking her hand, I say, "We're going home, and tomorrow we'll leave bright and early for the island."

She yanks her hand away and wails, putting her hands to her face. "Why are you doing this? I just want to see my friend and spend the night. Why did you have to come over here and ruin it?"

A car door slams outside. My heart pounds. Plum's mom could be coming home, and I don't want her to witness an embarrassing power struggle with my daughter, or for her to brand me as a bad mother.

I set the backpack on the floor, opening my hands. "Kelly, I'm sorry I came over here and ruined your time with your friend. But I didn't like the way you refused to go with me tomorrow, and I lost it. Let's move on and forget it. Forgive me?"

Her cheeks are wet with tears, and she sniffs, wiping her nose with the back of her hand. "Yeah. Of course. You're my mom."

I step over to her and wrap her in my arms. Her shoulder shake, and she sobs. I pat her back and whisper, "I'm sorry I lost my temper."

She moves away, wiping her eyes. "Do you really want me to go tomorrow?"

I nod. "I do. I want to hang out with you and have a fun day on the water, like we used to. Tex wants to see you too."

She brightens. "Can Plum come?"

I cock my head. "If her mom says it's okay."

Plum comes in the room. "I can't go. My mom needs me home tomorrow. We're going to a quilting circle with my grandmother."

I sigh, wishing my mother was alive. "Kels, are you okay if we go home now? It'll be easier for us to leave in the morning. And I'm sorry I sprung this on you all of a sudden."

She looks at Plum. "Sorry, I need to go home. You can eat my part of the pizza."

Her friend shrugs. "That's okay, I'll eat it for breakfast

tomorrow."

I head out the door with my daughter, my face blazing with heat at my failure to be a perfect parent. Climbing in the car, we buckle up, and I turn to Kelly. "I don't know what happened back there, but I turned into a monster. Maybe I need counselling, like I suggested for you. I'm so sorry."

She furrows her brow. "It was partly my fault for being stubborn. But I'm not your puppet to boss around. I want you to respect me. I'm not a little kid anymore."

Driving home, I say, "I get that. I think we're both rattled by my dad taking you. We could see the therapist Abby saw." I giggle and cover my mouth. "Do you remember her name?

Kelly chuckles. "Her name was Gladys Knight."

I burst into peals of laughter, and Kelly joins in. Gasping for breath, I say, "All she needed was Pips for her middle name."

We laugh, and I turn down our block but slow down when I see a police car parked in front of our house. An officer in blue stands on our front porch. A chill falls over our merry mood, and I pull in the driveway and park.

I murmur, "I wonder why the police are here."

We get out and hurry to the house.

8

JACKLYN

I sip steaming hot coffee with Mercury at the kitchen table and smile at how his cheeks are rosy from working outdoors on a winter day. Looking into the eyes of the kind man facing me brings to mind that the anniversary of my husband's death is looming next week. I blink back tears and sigh, feeling grateful for the good in my life.

Mercury sets down his mug and reaches across the table, taking my hand in his. "Everything okay?"

"Almost." I squeeze his warm hand. "I'm good and bad and a bit of a mess, because next week it will have been a year since Albert died. I loved him and trusted him, but he kept secrets from me, and so did my son. The last year of challenges was something I never wanted. But then a good thing is, I met you. I guess I'm just rattled with the anniversary of his death coming up."

He nods. "Is this what you would call a fruit basket upset?"

I chuckle. "Yes, and it's a big beautiful mess. I'm glad to have you as my friend."

He stands and gives me a soft kiss on the lips. "I'm here for it all. I think we make a good team."

Wiping tears away, I say, "I do too."

Buddy barks at the back door, and his hackles are up. We go to the window and look out at two raccoons in a fir tree. A big one sits on the ground, staring at my neighbor's place.

Buddy yips and runs through the house, looking out windows and growling.

Mercury and I hurry to the front window, and I clap a hand to my chest, counting raccoons walking past. One, two, three, four, five, six raccoons scurry by, heading to Zoila's place next door.

I shake my head. "She's feeding raccoons over there. I've seen them sitting in a semi-circle waiting to be fed on her front lawn at noon and six o'clock. She hand feeds them."

Mercury tugs on his long gray beard. "There's a new state rule that says you can't do that. Wildlife has to stand on its own and not have handouts from humans. You should tell her to stop."

I put my hands on my hips. "I did, but she doesn't care. She said she deserves to do whatever she wants."

"Talk to her again. It's not healthy to have this many

raccoons in one place. I think we just saw nine of them in the space of five minutes."

I stare out the front window. "Buddy could get hurt. I'll go talk to her again."

"Want me to go with you?"

I kiss his cheek. "No thanks, I'll be fine. Just be sure Buddy doesn't get out when I leave. I'm worried they'll attack him."

My pulse picks up, and I pull on my coat, grab a walking stick and step outside, inhaling a heady scent of salt air coming off Cedar Channel. I take a deep breath to calm myself, because it won't go any good to cause a dust up with my next-door neighbor. I'm already prickly with her because she stole my firewood on Christmas Eve, so she's not winning points with me.

I walk away from the house, and Buddy barks at the window. Clutching the wooden walking stick, I stop on the sidewalk, staring next door.

Zoila is wearing a long midnight blue velvet robe with the hood pulled up. Six raccoons with adorable bandit faces sit on their back feet on the front lawn. She holds a white bowl in her hands, and the raccoons watch her every move.

She bends and puts circle-shaped sugary cereal in outstretched paws. "There you go," she says in a soft voice. "Call me Auntie."

I grit my teeth and bide my time until her ritual ends. It won't do me any good to charge in with wild animals close at hand and spark an angry confrontation, even though I'd like to.

Zoila tips over the empty bowl and wiggles her fingers. "It's all gone, Bye."

Raccoons drift away, and I clear my throat, stepping carefully over to her. "Zoila, I'd like to speak with you."

She pouts her full red lips. "Isn't that what we're doing right now?"

"Raccoons can carry disease and be dangerous, especially to dogs, like my Buddy. Your feeding them has brought more raccoons here, and it's not healthy. There's a new state rule that prohibits feeding wildlife."

She cocks her head, putting a hand on her hip. Mist drifts down, and droplets sparkle on her long brown hair, making her more beautiful. "Aren't you high and mighty? Here I was, feeling a wee bit better about my being sick, but you squashed my good mood like a gnat. Thanks, Jackie, for bringing me down."

I cross my arms. "My name is Jacklyn, not Jackie.

She smiles. "Hit a soft spot, did I, Jackie? Well, don't worry, I won't be seeing you much, so I don't have to remember what to call you except Debbie Downer. It's just me and the raccoons over here, hanging out and having a good time without you."

"The entire neighborhood is impacted by what you're doing. Raccoons are tipping over trash cans and congregating in our yards. It isn't all about what you want."

Her mouth falls open. "You want my suggestion? Go

look in the mirror, because you charged over here all upset. Get a bigger life. I'm helping wild creatures survive, but you're running around worrying about your precious pet."

Fire might as well be blazing out of my eyes when I stare at her. A million mean retorts run through my mind but I press my lips together.

She opens her arms, gesturing to raccoons watching us from fifteen feet away. "You do you, and I'll do me. But don't come over and tell me what to do again."

I tighten my grip on the walking stick. "Just so you know, I'm calling animal control." I turn and stride away, wind whipping past my cheeks.

She calls, "Good neighbors don't act like this. They get along."

I roll my eyes and hurry to the safety of my home, where my new friend waits with my dog Buddy. My neighbor across the street, Bernard Frackus, stands at his window, watching, and I wave to him. He adjusts his black-framed glasses and nods.

I rush in the house and slam the door shut behind me. Mercury locks it and says with a smile, "To keep out the vermin and varmints."

I pull off my coat, hanging it up. "Not to mention troublemakers, like my son." Pointing next door, I say, "That woman is on her own planet. What I said didn't make a dent, and she said she won't stop feeding the raccoons."

He shrugs. "Everyone sees the world through different lenses."

"If it keeps on like this, we'll soon be outnumbered. Raccoons one-hundred, Jacklyn one. I'm calling animal control."

An operator connects me to an animal control officer. I explain the situation, and she says, "The new rule in our state is to reduce unnatural concentrations of deer, elk and moose. Raccoons are a nuisance animal. There's no law against feeding raccoons."

"But there are more and more of them."

"You can call a trapper. Look online for contact information for approved trappers on the State Fish and Wildlife website."

"I'm not ready to hire a trapper. They're innocent animals, and it's not their fault someone is feeding them and attracting them here. Will you take some raccoons and move them to another area?"

"No, we can't do that. It would just relocate the problem. Besides, there's no law against feeding the raccoons."

I thank her and hang up, rubbing my temples, and say to Mercury, "No help there. We're on our own with the raccoons."

He smiles. "Maybe six of them isn't such a big deal."

I tap a finger to my lips. "Or was it nine? I guess we'll have to live with it."

He says with a sparkle in his eyes, "With all the ruckus

going on outside, we're safe and snug in your bungalow, tucked inside with each other."

Buddy nuzzles my leg, and I pet his soft ears. "Don't forget about Buddy. He's part of the family too."

A raccoon scurries past outside, followed by two more, and Buddy barks.

Mercury opens his arms, and I step into his warmth, wrapping my arms around him. I didn't want to start a new life, but a new adventure was forced upon me. Listening to his steady heartbeat, I'm grateful to have Mercury in my life, and I have much to do.

9

IRENA

 stout middle-aged police officer adjusts his wire-rimmed glasses. "Are you Irena Fishbone?"

My throat closes tight. "Yes, that's me. Is anything wrong?"

"May I come inside? I have a few questions for you."

Happy, the dog we're watching for friends, barks, and I nudge him aside, telling him to sit.

I gesture to an armchair by the fireplace. "What's this about?"

He sits, and the chair creaks. Kelly and I perch on the couch.

Watching me closely as if looking for a reaction, he says, "We're investigating an accident to determine if it was a vehicular homicide. The driver was your friend Abby Love."

I clap a hand to my mouth. "Oh no. People died in the accident?"

He nods.

I whoosh out a breath. "I'm sorry to hear that. How is Abby doing?"

"Her condition is stable, but she has some broken bones. When I interviewed her, she said she was driving to the town of Lancer to see if a girl in an altercation at a store was your daughter. She seemed to imply that the reason she was driving so fast in hazardous conditions was because you urged her to go, despite the snow storm. Is that correct?"

I glance at Kelly, sitting beside me. Her hands are trembling, and I put an arm around her shaking shoulders. "Kelly, do you need to go to your room? It might be traumatic for you to revisit the night when you were taken."

She crosses her arms. "It's okay. I want to hear what he says."

I turn to the officer. "I wanted to go to Lancer to see if my missing daughter was there, but FBI agents told me to stay here, in case Kelly came home. And Abby volunteered to go. She wanted to make the trip and said her car would be fine in the snow."

He cocks his head. "Was she on the phone with you when she had the accident? We're checking her phone records, but that'll take a while."

I frown. "No, and as far as I know, she didn't call

anyone. She's a good driver and very careful. I think this is her first accident."

He shakes his head. "Are you aware your friend Abby Love has had multiple citations for speeding?"

My eyebrows shoot up. "I had no idea."

Kelly leans into me, and I squeeze her shoulder. "I don't see how I can be of any more help to you. Abby has a big heart, and if she was driving faster than she should've in a snow storm, it was because she loves my daughter. Will that be all?"

He rises and tips his hat. "Thank you for answering my questions. I'll see myself out."

He gently closes the door, and rain taps on the window panes. If only we could go back to the way we were, but that won't ever happen. We've been branded by traumatic events, like my ex-husband being pursued by a debt collector, a boating accident, and Kelly's abduction. Our worlds went way off-kilter, and we must adjust, if we hope to find any peace.

Kelly sobs in my arms, and I pat her back, while Happy the dog rubs up against us. She pulls away and says, "What will Dad do without Abby taking care of him? He needs her."

I arch an eyebrow. "He'll help her, and it'll be good for him to take care of someone else. I hope he'll step up and get trained for a job and keep it for once."

"Dad's not a very good role model, given the mistakes he's made, but I love him."

I nod. "I love him too, just as a friend."

Just then, my phone rings, and I see Jack is calling.

I'm about to answer when Kelly moans and rolls her eyes. "Not the phone. You're always on the phone for your job. I hate it."

I look into her eyes. "It's your father, so let's see what he has to say."

10

DUSTY

As I drive toward my new digs in a musty cabin near the mountains, I get an idea and stop at a bar. I want to see a guy who gave me fireworks to use at my mom's place to shake her up. I smile, because that rattled her cage.

I stride inside, shove my hands in my pockets and look around in dim light. He waves to me from the billiards table, and I nod, stopping to order a beer at the bar. Holding a cold bottle in my hand, I go over and watch him shoot pool. Like most men in the place, we're dressed in plaid flannel shirts, jeans and work boots, ready to work outdoors.

When the pool table is clear except for the cue ball, he pulls off his blue ball cap, runs a hand through his brown hair and says, "How's it going? Did the fireworks go off?

They were in my trunk so long; I was worried they wouldn't work."

A smile spreads across my face. "Oh, yeah, they went off. Freaked everyone out and took them by surprise. They came pouring out of the house, and I got them good."

He takes a swig of his beer, and I plunge ahead with my plan. Clearing my throat, I say, "Any interest in joining me in a fake home invasion, where we'd go in and scare my mom, just for fun? It's going to be a belated Christmas gift, because she asked me to spring a surprise on her and do something dramatic, so she'll feel more alive."

When he looks hesitant, I add, "It's kind of crazy, I know, but she requested it."

He cocks his head. "Sounds strange, if you ask me. No thanks, that's not my kind of thing."

"Come on, it won't be a big deal. We'll dress in black and wear facemasks, so she won't recognize us. We'll scare the living daylights out of her. She loves a good fright."

He frowns. "Won't we get in trouble? What if she calls the police and says it's a home invasion?"

I open my arms, plastering on a charming smile. "She loves scary movies and surprises. It'll be fun. Come on, man."

"All right. But I don't want to get into trouble. You sure it's okay?"

I nod. "Absolutely, no question. We'll head over there tonight and pop in when she's asleep."

He shrugs and racks the pool balls. "Fine, I'm in. What time will we leave?"

I rub my right cheek. "We'll take off in separate cars at nine o'clock. By the time we get to Millersville, it'll be ten or so, the perfect time to bust open her front door."

He flinches, and his pool stick almost falls to the floor, but he catches it in time. "Sounds like you're planning to break in, and I'm not up for that. Let's use your key instead. We'll be quiet and stealth-like, and then shazam, wake her up all of a sudden." He waves his hands in the air and smiles. "Surprise, Mom. We're here."

I make a sour face. "I don't have a key."

His eyes open wide. "You don't have a key to your mother's place?"

My face heats, and I burn with an angry flame of resentment, fueled by an eternal shame she dished out during my childhood. I was the unseen family member at the dinner table, when Mom and Dad crowed about my sister's accomplishments. Now it's time for me to get back at her for how I lived in the shadows and never met her expectations. Revenge is my favorite meal, served with a side dish of thwarting her success. She'll want to surrender my company by the time I'm done, with the assistance of my new friend.

With a shrug, I say, "I don't have a key, but this will make it more realistic. She was watching the news the other night and said she wondered what a home invasion was like, so we've got to stage it down to the last detail."

He nods, scratching his beard. "Okay, it sounds like fun. Let's do this." He holds out a hand.

I blow out a breath, glad to have a sidekick joining me, because if things go sideways, he'll take the blame. Shaking on it, I say, "We're ready, man."

He points to the racked balls on green felt. "You break?"

"Sure."

I pick up a pool stick and aim, sending the white cue ball into a solid orange. Colorful balls spread out on the table, just like my spider web plans for the future. One by one, I'll pocket my successes and win my company back, picking up cash along the way. I deserve to have my mother's money, and I've found a willing victim to invade her home. Everything is going my way.

11

JACKLYN

Mercury says goodbye for the night and heads to his place to help his new roommate, Del, who left Shore Lodge with us on Irena's boat on Christmas Eve. He's living in Mercury's violin workshop in a room with bunk beds. I shake my head at how Dusty showed up uninvited that night and tried to convince my friends that my memory is impaired. Memory problems, my left foot. I'm as sharp as ever, and he'll learn that the next time he tries any hijinks.

I let my beagle-mix dog out the back door before we go to bed, and I step outside to watch him. Briny sea air laden with the promise of rain wafts past. A pack of coyotes howl on a nearby hill, and their yipping, growling sounds send shivers up my spine. Two sets of eyes blink by bushes, where raccoons must be watching us. Goosebumps prick my flesh, and I rub my arms.

When he's done his business, I call, "Come on, don't dally. It's wild out tonight."

Buddy runs inside and shakes. I close the door and lock it, letting out a sigh of relief. No one will bother us tonight. We're safe, and soon we'll be tucked in bed fast asleep.

Buddy trots to the bedroom, and I shuffle down the hall, slippers slapping on the wood floor. "Well, sweet dog, we've avoided Dusty's devious tricks for a few days, which make us lucky indeed. Off to bed we go."

Buddy turns in a circle on his bed on the floor and curls up, white-tipped tail tucked under his nose.

I climb into bed and pull up the covers, wide awake and listening for unusual noises. The coyotes calling put me on edge. My last thoughts before I draft off to sleep are of my son. Tomorrow, I will prepare for whatever his next attack will be. I must anticipate his every move.

My eyes open in the dark. Dusty might speak to the commercial loan officer at my bank to scuttle their approving my loan for Stone Estates. He could bad-mouth me to potential investors, who own businesses in the area. I'd better watch out, because there are many ways he could go behind my back and sabotage my success.

12

─────────

DUSTY

y the time we stagger out of the bar, I'm swaying from drinking beers. Crisp cold night air snaps me to my senses, and I say to my new buddy, "Here's the plan. Follow me to Millersville, and we'll park a block from my mom's place. It's a yellow bungalow. You can't miss it. A big tree feel down in her front yard during the storm on Christmas Eve."

He nods and yawns. "Hope this won't take too long. I've got to get up early tomorrow morning."

"Why is that?"

He shrugs. "I run the grocery store in town, and I open early every morning."

"Can you give me a job? I'm looking."

He crosses his arms. "What kind of experience do you have? Do you know how to ring up sales and stock shelves? Deal with customers?"

I shake my head. "Not really, but I could learn. My area of expertise is in construction. I build custom homes."

His mouth drops open. "That pays a whole lot more than what I'd pay. Stick with construction. You'll be a wealthy man, my friend."

I resist the urge to roll my eyes. "Hasn't worked out that way for me, not yet."

He slaps my back. "You never know. Keep with it. Don't give up."

I rest a hand on my chest, burying sadness and regretting what I've lost since my dad died. "Hey, what's your name anyway? I forgot."

He touches the rim of his ballcap. "Bubba."

"I'm Dusty. Okay, let's go."

We climb in our trucks and I take off, peeling out of the gravel parking lot. I'm wounded, restless and reckless. He follows me, and I grin, heading for Highway 20.

Rain patters down on the windshield, but it doesn't dampen my mood. We're headed to my hometown, where I intend to leave my mark behind.

Roaring down the road, we honk our horns and yell into the dark night. I scream along with a rock song on the radio and slow down when I enter Millersville, turning off the music. No need to get ticketed for speeding or thrown in jail for reckless driving.

I turn down Mom's street and creep along at ten miles an hour, pulling over to the curb a few houses away from hers. I gently close my truck door, so as not to make a loud noise, but Bubba parks behind me and jumps out, slamming his door shut.

I put a finger in front of my lips to shush him, but he breaks into laughter, bending over and grabbing his knees. A giggle escapes my lips, and soon the two of us are slapping our thighs and laughing like kids.

Finally, I wipe my eyes. "Whew, I haven't laughed like that in a long time."

He chuckles. "Me neither, man. Where's your mom's house?"

I whisper and point. "It's the yellow bungalow over there. I'll grab a face mask for you. I'll wear a motorcycle helmet, so she won't know who it is."

He turns toward his truck but stops. "You sure about this, buddy? It seems like a crazy idea, now that I'm sobering up. Maybe we should just go home and forget it."

My pulse quickens, and I wave a hand in the air. "Don't think. Just do it. We'll laugh about it later. She asked for it."

He studies a patch of ground illuminated by a street light.

To nudge him, I say, "It'll be fun. She likes to be scared. Just pretend you're in a horror movie, playing a role."

He eyes me and smiles. "When you put it that way, okay, let's get it done."

13

JACKLYN

A loud thump in the living room wakes me, and I jump out of bed, running to trouble. Buddy roars into the room, barking his head off and baring his teeth. Wood splinters, and the front door flies open, slamming against the wall.

My pulse is pounding. Punching a button on the smart watch Mercury gave me, I alert the police to an emergency. I grab a candlestick and heft it in my hands as a weapon.

Two tall men in black jackets and jeans enter my house. One wears a motorcycle helmet, and a second one in a black face mask brandishes a can of what looks like bear spray.

Adrenaline courses through my body, and my hands tremble. I hold up the heavy metal candlestick and face the two men, screaming, "Get out. Get out, or I'll hurt you."

Cold air rushes in the room, rippling through my flannel pajamas. My knees shake. Buddy latches onto the face-masked man's jeans, tugging and growling.

Counting the minutes until the police arrive, I clutch the candlestick, ready to protect my dog by hitting the home invaders on the head. "Get out. I called the police."

The man with a face mask chuckles, holding up a can of bear spray. "Surprise."

Behind him, a raccoon comes up the front path and sits on its back feet in the doorway, chittering and begging.

I yell, "Get out of my house!"

The man in the motorcycle helmet laughs and runs toward the study, but I stick out my leg and trip him. He falls flat on his face on the wood floor, moaning. I whack him over the shoulders and back with the candle stick, and he goes still. Scanning the room, I take rope I used to teach Mercury how to tie knots for boating and whip his hands behind his back, tying him up in a flash.

The other man tries to shake off Buddy, who is biting his ankle. He cries out and he's not laughing any longer. He holds up a can of bear spray, but before he gets off a shot, I throw the candlestick at his head, and it hits the mark. The raccoon turns and runs off into the yard.

The man howls, drops the bear spray and runs outside just as a Millersville squad car pulls up. Two officers climb out, and one apprehends the face masked man, cuffing him on the spot. The other officer hurries toward the house.

I slump to the floor and wrap my trembling arms around Buddy, who is panting. I'm breathing hard too. He leans against me, and I pet his soft fur. My heart hammers hard, and I wish I could fly away from my troubles. What fresh hell is this, where two men broke into my house?

A young officer's eyes grow wide, studying a man on the floor with his hands tied behind his back. "What happened? Are you okay?"

I point to the man on the floor. His motorcycle helmet flew off when I tripped him. "Two men broke in my home, and this one is my son."

I stumble on weak legs over to a floor lamp and turn on a light. Before we can discuss details, Zoila, my new next-door neighbor appears in the doorway, wearing a white negligee under a royal blue velvet floor-length robe with black boots. Her eyes latch onto Dusty, and she says, "Everything all right? I heard a commotion and came to see if you're okay."

I purse my lips because there is something strange and suspicious about this new neighbor. Her eyes flit about the room and land on the can of bear spray. For all I know, Dusty might have contacted her to see if my lights were off, to make sure I was asleep before he tried his ugly trick. They could be in cahoots, because they sure were cozy with each other on Christmas Eve, almost like they knew each other before they first met in front of my house. I'll have to look into her when I have time.

Her faltering smile turns into a snarl for a fleeting second before she makes her expression blank. Her perfect eyebrows arch, and she stares at my son's broad back.

My muscles tense, and every nerve jangles, calling for flight or fight, but instead I got fright. I doubt she gives a wooden nickel about how I'm faring after the toe-curling ordeal Buddy and I just experienced.

I glance at Buddy to be sure he's okay and say, "My son broke into my house to assault me, so I'm not doing well, but thanks for asking. And you can bet I'll press charges. This incident will not be forgotten. But thanks for checking on me. I appreciate it."

Her eyes linger on Dusty, who is knocked out. "I'll leave you to it. I just wanted to check and see how you're doing." She gives a little wave and turns swiftly, her flowing blue robe swirling around her, before disappearing into the dark night.

I turn to the officer. "Thank you for getting here so quickly. I was terrified. I can't believe this happened."

An older officer puts the face-masked man in the squad car and marches into the house, eyeing the living room. Dim light casts shadows, showing dark smudges below his eyes. He says, "We'll take them in and book them. Was anything taken?"

I shake my head. "No, they didn't have a chance to get that far. But I think my son was heading to my study."

Dusty groans on the floor. "You can't prove anything. This was meant to be a fun surprise. You asked what a home invasion was like, and I went out of my way to set up a pretend one and show you."

The officers haul Dusty to his feet, and the older one says, "That's a good story, but I'm not buying it."

Dusty splutters. "She asked me to do this. I was only acting out what she wanted. Seriously, officers, this isn't what it looks like. Not at all."

I say, "You're delusional. I would never ask you to do something this crazy."

I blow out a breath and try to slow my racing heart. I don't want to have a heart attack, like my husband. I wipe my sweaty hands on my pajamas.

The older officer handcuffs Dusty and says, "Let's go."

Dusty glares at me. "I'll be back. This isn't the end of it."

I scowl. "This is a bridge too far, and I hope they charge you with everything on the books. I hope you like small rooms with bars for doors."

They walk out, and I hold Buddy by the collar as he growls at a raccoon on my front lawn. The officers put my son in a squad car and drive off, and I shake my head at how my family has become a battle ground, with a fight raging between right and wrong.

Picking up my phone, I dial my friend Mercury's number.

He answers, saying in a sleepy voice, "Jacklyn? What's wrong?"

I swallow and my throat is dry. "Two men broke in my house. Dusty did it."

"I'll be right over. Hang on tight."

14

ZOILA

I peer out the window and watch two police officers march Dusty to a squad car, put him in the back and drive away. I smile, because this is a perfect opportunity to set my plan in motion to get my ex-husband Kirk to pay my medical bills and win him back. I'll help Dusty, using him as bait, which I bet will make Kirk jealous.

I pick up the phone and call Kirk, who lives next door with his second wife. They've been married for three years, and I figure it's time to push them apart and reap the rewards.

When he answers, I say in a sing-song voice, "I'm sorry to call this late, but I was hoping to find you in because I need a little favor. You know that money you promised me for my medical bills? Could I have it tonight? Something's come up."

He whispers. "Why in the hell would you call me this late at night? Don't call me at home ever again. And why would you think I have money like that on hand?"

I croon, "Oh, come on. We're friends. There's nothing wrong with a phone call."

In the background, I hear his wife say, "Who are you talking to? Come back to bed."

I say in a soothing tone, the counterpoint to his wife's grating sound, "Please, Kirk, I really need your help. I know I depend on you so much but without you, I'd just wither up and die." I roll my eyes at the last part, which is laying it on thick, but he'll lap it up.

He whispers, "I'll Venmo you the money in a few minutes." He hangs up.

I push on a cuticle and plot my next move. Pulling off my wig, I breathe out a sigh of relief. The wig makes my head hot and itch.

In the bathroom, I look in the mirror, examining hairs sprouting on my scalp. I take a razor, lather up shaving cream and shave my head. Blotting my head with a towel, I smile at the mirror. "Go claim what's yours."

15

KIRK

I set down the phone after talking to Zoila and wipe my brow. I promised I'd help her through cancer treatments, but my wife would kill me if she knew. My heart thuds, and I clench my hands. I have to get through the next few weeks and then everything will settle down.

I transfer the money I promised Zoila and head to bed, but as I shuffle down the hall, I deeply regret getting mixed up with my manipulating ex-wife. I have no choice but to keep my word, or she'll tell my wife about the money I embezzled at my first job. My cheeks heat with shame, and I head to bed. It's a relief to be married to my second wife, who lacks a hidden agenda.

I swallow hard and slip into bed, pulling up the covers. My wife is snoring, so I turn on my side, facing away from her. Closing my eyes, I try to sleep but worry keeps me awake. I can't let my wife find out I'm helping Zoila with her bills. I made a huge mistake when I fell under my ex-wife's spell and became bewitched by the woman next door. Why I suggested she move in next to us is beyond me. I must have been out of my mind.

16

MERCURY

I leave Del sleeping at my place and rush to my car. He's been staying with me until he finds a long-term living situation. Rain patters down, hitting a bald spot on my head, and I start the car, but Del comes running out, slamming the door shut and waving his arms.

He opens the passenger door and hops in the shotgun seat. "I heard you on the phone. Is Jacklyn in trouble? I want to help. Let's go."

I pull away from the curb and drive away. "There was an unfortunate incident at her house."

"What happened?"

"Dusty staged a home invasion at her house. He broke in."

Del wipes a hand down his face. "That's awful. How frightening for her."

I nod. "Her son is out of control. We need to rein him in, if the police don't do it."

Del frowns. "I'll help. This isn't right. She deserves to live her life in peace. Especially after all her son put her through, admitting her to Shore Lodge."

I turn down Jacklyn's street. "I agree. Talk about a screwed-up family."

Del cocks his head. "You should see mine, if you want to see tension and a real screwed up family."

I wince. "Sounds like something I'd rather not see up close."

His chuckle is forced. "Yeah, that's why I'm keeping my distance from my brother."

I park in front of Jacklyn's, and we hop out, hurrying to her house.

She runs into my open arms, and I pat her back. Del turns away, wiping his eyes.

I step back. "Tell me what he did."

She explains how two men broke in and scared the living daylights out of her, and I begin to form a plan to straighten out her son. A ton of possibilities flit through my mind. We could run him out of town. Ruin his name, so he'll never work here again. Drop him off on an isolated island, so he can't get back. I'll mull these ideas over later and figure out the best approach to solving the problem of devastating, devious Dusty, who thinks only of himself.

17

DUSTY

Sweat trickles down my arms, and my body odor reeks of fear. Grabbing hold of cold metal jail cell bars, I yank on them with all my might. "Let me out." I bellow and issue a stream of swear words, but no one comes.

"Rough day, huh?" I turn around and glare at a long-haired grizzled old man.

"You could say that, yeah." I put my hands on my hips and wipe my wet mouth on the back of my hand.

"What did you do?"

I shake my head. "Don't want to talk about. It's not my fault. They misunderstood the situation."

My cellmate says, "That's what everyone says."

"I'm different. I didn't do anything."

A guard comes by and nods to me. "Someone here to see you."

My pulse picks up, and I wheel around, hoping to see my sister ready to bail me out or our family friend Fred, who is an attorney. Instead, I see Zoila saunter down the cell block. Men behind bars whistle, and she extenuates the sway of her hips. She's dressed in a red low-cut V-neck dress that flares from the waist.

She leans in and puckers her red lips. "Miss me?"

I clear my throat. She is a seductress, but she's not after me. She wants the man who lives next-door to her, the one who is happily re-married and who happens to be Zoila's ex-husband. I say in a hoarse voice, "Uh huh."

She smiles, putting a hand on her hip. "Well, today is your lucky day. I posted your bail."

My jaw drops. I'll owe her big time, and this is a woman I don't want to be in debt to. She's ruthless and gets what she wants, including every man she's set her eyes on. "I guess I should say thanks."

"I'll give you a ride back to my place when they release you. You'll stay with me, and your job is to make my ex-husband seethe with jealousy."

I cringe. "I don't want to get in the middle of whatever is going on between you and your ex-husband. Leave me out of it. I'll find my way home."

She points a red lacquered fingernail at me. "Oh, no you don't. I'm calling the shots now, and you owe me. You'll do what I ask until I say otherwise."

I gulp, and my throat is as parched as kiln-dried lumber.

The guy from the bar who helped me with the failed fake home invasion calls from the next cell. "Don't leave me holding the bag. This whole thing was your idea. You were the mastermind behind the prank. You asked me to go with you."

A guard says, "Calm down. Getting upset won't do you any good. Save it for your lawyer and when you're in court."

My buddy the pool player grips the bars. His flushed face is wet with beads of sweat. "It isn't fair what you did. You tricked me and you're saying it was my idea. But it wasn't. I'll never let you in my grocery store again. Don't show your face in Foothills. I spread word in town and you'll be a pariah. Watch your back, because I'll be coming after you."

A guard unlocks my jail cell and swings the door open. I step out, rubbing my wrists. I shrug at the man I shafted by bringing him in on my plan. "Whatever. See you later."

He yells, "You'll regret what you did, talking me into this. You're going down."

Zoila takes my arm, and we walk away. She looks over and whispers. "That friend of yours you just left in the lurch? Never treat me like that, or you'll regret it."

My chest tightens with fear. Just when I was heading for freedom, she roped me in and wrapped me around her finger. I hope I can survive the next few months, with all of these people out to get me.

18

MERCURY

Del and I help Jacklyn put up a piece of plywood over her front door and screw it in place using a power screwdriver. While we're working, a car drives up next door, and my jaw drops when Dusty climbs out of the car.

He glances over and nods to me, and my hands clench. I'm itching to see justice done, and he needs to be taught a lesson about respecting his mother and the law. Only a crazy person would invade a loved one's home, scaring the living daylights out of them. I doubt he feels love, like the rest of us do, and I bet he just sees her as a way to bankroll his lifestyle, spitting out dollar bills. Whatever is going on, there's definitely something wrong with Jacklyn's grown son.

Jacklyn glares at Dusty, putting her hands on her hips. "I can't believe they let him out of jail. I'm tempted to go over there and slap him for what he did to Buddy and me, scaring us senseless in our own home. Someone must have posted his bail. And what's he doing next door? He sure got friendly with Zoila fast."

Del shakes his head. "I bet he's a magnet for women. I was never like that."

I say, "If they knew what he was really like inside, they'd run away."

Jacklyn crosses her arms and watches Zoila saunter, arm in arm, with Dusty to her house. "My son landed in a bed of roses, without the thorns. You'd think being a pariah in his hometown would make him stay away, but he keeps coming back."

I press my lips together and don't say a word. I'm cooking up a scheme to straighten out her son, and if she has no knowledge of what will take place, she won't take the blame.

I drive Del back to my place, let him in and return to Jacklyn's to stand watch for the night. Her dog curls up on the living room rug, spent from his efforts protecting Jacklyn when Dusty broke in. Jacklyn paces the floor, wringing her hands.

She says in a low, trembling voice, "I've never been so scared in all my life. Not even when I was in my kayak in strong currents and thought I might die."

I take her in my arms, and she weeps, shoulders shuddering. I murmur in her ear, "Everything's going to be all right. We'll get through this together."

She lets out a sigh. "Let head to bed. We can cuddle."

I shake my head. "I'll tuck you in, but I'll stay on watch out here. I don't feel safe with Dusty next door."

She releases a whoosh of breath. "Thanks."

I tuck her into bed, kiss her cheek and go into the living room, turning off the lights. Pulling a blanket around my shoulders, I sit on the sofa, lean back against a cushion and plot my revenge. I'll do whatever it takes to protect Jacklyn and keep her safe. After all she's been through, with her husband dying and her discovering his secrets, and Dusty putting her in Shore Lodge and invading her home, she deserves a happy life. I'll do the best I can to give her that.

19

———

KIRK

Hearing a noise, I slip out of bed and part the curtains, peering out a window. I chew on my lip and stare at the house I rented for Zoila, an expense my wife knows nothing about.

A car door slams, and my wife stirs in bed. My jaw drops when Zoila walks arm in arm with a tall, broad-shouldered man. I cuss under my breath. How could she do this to me? I'm paying her expenses, and she's taking on a new boyfriend? That isn't right.

My wife sits up. "What is it? Is something going on next door?"

"Nothing." I wave a hand in the air, like it's no big deal, but I've been betrayed. I helped my ex-wife by providing shelter during a tough time and wrongly assumed she'd keep to herself while protecting my secret. For her to flaunt a romantic relationship under my nose makes my skin crawl.

I climb into bed, and my wife says, "Is something bothering you? You seem distracted lately and obsessed with watching what's going on next door."

I shrug. "It's all good."

She reaches for my hand, squeezing it. "Are you still in love with her?"

My pulse picks up, and my body turns cold. I hold my breath. She can't find out.

She says, "If you are, you have to pick between us."

I say in a soft voice, "You've got it all wrong. I'm just helping a friend. Let's go back to sleep."

I pull my hand away, close my eyes and suddenly realize I have feelings for the woman next door. I've been trying to ignore them, but on this dark night, it is clear. I love two women at once, which isn't fair to either of them. This won't work for me or them, and I've got to find a way to wiggle out of the mess I cooked up for myself.

20

IRENA

The next morning, I let Abby and Jack's dog out in the yard. He's staying with us until they get back on their feet and can walk him. He does his business and bounds back inside, licking my hand. Patting his head, I wince at how I acted with Kelly yesterday when I insisted she leave her friend's house right away. I've got to be less strident and strict with her, because she deserves all the compassion and understanding I can dredge up, after what she went through.

Checking the time, I pad down the hall and knock on Kelly's door. "Rise and shine. We're off to Grand Island this morning. I know you love boat rides."

When no answer comes, I say, "We'll eat breakfast before we go. Come on, Kels."

I stand at the door, listening for the sound of Kelly

moving in the room and hear nothing. Not wanting to be a witch of a mother, I wait. Tick, tick, tick, goes my heart.

After what feels like forever but was a few minutes, I say, "I'm coming in."

I put my hand on the cool metal door knob and turn it, slowly opening the door. I smile at the lump in the bed that is my beloved sleeping daughter. Sitting on the side of the bed, I gently shake her shoulder. "Hey, sleepy head. Time to wake up."

Happy the dog hops on the bed and licks her face.

She moans. "Leave me alone. Let me sleep."

"Hey, I made pancakes. I've got the batter ready."

She opens an eye. "Pancakes?"

I nod. "Yep, all you have to do is get out of bed, and I'll start cooking them."

"Do we have maple syrup?"

I smile. "We do." Patting her back, I rise and say, "See you in the kitchen."

She groans. "Okay."

I step out of the room and smile, because my loving daughter has returned this morning. Heating the griddle, I add oil and flick a drop of water at it. When it sizzles in the pan, I pour in pancake batter.

Kelly shuffles into the kitchen wearing a robe and slippers. She yawns, putting a hand over her open mouth, and stops at the refrigerator, pouring a glass of orange juice.

Sliding three golden-brown pancakes onto a plate, I

set her breakfast on the table. "Ta da. A masterpiece, just for you."

She rolls her eyes and sits at the kitchen table. "Thanks."

I grin at my sweet girl and pour pancake batter on the griddle. While they sizzle and cook, I go over and give my daughter the biggest hug, coming up from behind. "I love you, hon."

She stops eating mid-bite, fork in the air, and pulls away. "Ick, Mom, I'm eating. Not now."

I swallow a lump in my throat, missing what is gone. With a sigh, I remind myself our boat has sailed from the dock, and we're headed to a new future, whether I like it or not.

21

KELLY

Mom and I leave the house, acting like we always do when we're heading to the boat. Driving toward the marina with the dog in the back, she acts like nothing has changed, but inside, I feel strange, like a new part of myself emerged after my grandfather took me. I barely know who I am now.

At the marina, Happy jumps out, and I walk him on a leash through the marina, letting him stop at bushes along the way. We board the boat, check the oil and warm up the engine, shrugging on life vests. Happy smiles when I snap buckles shut on his life vest.

Mom grins, eyes wide. "Ready, first mate?"

Despite my uneasy mood, I can't help but smile back. "Ready."

"Cast off the lines."

I hustle from the wheelhouse and untie dock lines,

coiling them in my hands and setting them onboard to take with us. Pushing off from the dock, I hop onboard and say, "Lines are off. Let's go."

She puts the boat in gear, and we're off for another adventure on the water. Mom owns a boat rescue business, and boaters in distress call her day and night. It's pretty dramatic when she runs racing from the house at all hours to stop boats from sinking and towing them to the marina or shipyard. If the Coast Guard can't make it in time, she's the one who roars away from the marina to pull people from a sinking ship. She wants me to follow in her footsteps and take over the business one day, but I have other things I want to do, like move to Seattle and enroll in dance classes.

Wind whips past my cheeks, and I make a face, because with all that's been going on with my dad going missing and how he owed a ton of money to dangerous people, I haven't been to dance class in a while. I shrug and look up at the Cap Sante Viewpoint, waving to people standing on the bluff. Maybe I don't want to dance anymore. The night Grandad took me stole my joy, and I'm not sure how to get it back.

I go back in the wheelhouse and take my seat, buckling in for the ride. Mom's boat goes fast, and I used to love the feeling of flying across the waves, water splashing over the bow and up the sides. Now, I'm blah inside and not looking forward to the ride ahead.

Mom says, "Buckled in?"

"Yeah."

She pushes on the throttle. "Here we go."

We head into Fidalgo Bay, and she turns the wheel, heading north to Cedar Channel. We're bucking the current, but that doesn't matter much in Mom's boat, with her powerful engines. Gliding past Shore Lodge, looming to our right on Cedar Island, Mom says, "Tex asked to see you, and I wanted to spend the day with you, so that's why I insisted you come along."

I can see my breath in the cool air inside the cabin, so I say, "Can you turn on the heat? I'm cold."

"Sure thing." She flicks a switch and turns up the volume on the marine radio.

"I owe Tex," Mom says, "for how she helped out when a debt collector was going to hurt your dad."

"I can see that. But I wish we didn't have to go all the way to Grand Island to talk to her. How long will this take? I want to go back to town to see my friends."

"I don't know how long it'll take. A few hours?"

I shift in my seat and roll my eyes. "A few hours?"

She glances at me and looks ahead as we approach Rosario Strait. A Washington State ferry chugs along, heading south, and a wisp of fog rises over the water to the north.

"All clear," she says, steering northwest across the strait that smugglers used during prohibition to carry people, drugs and alcohol in boats without lights, running dark at night. Mom says, "Who are these friends you mentioned? I thought Plum was your friend."

I shrug. "No one special, but I might want to hang out with new people for a change."

She swallows and frowns. "Okay, I guess. But remember old friends are the best."

I tilt my head. "I know you think that, being so close to Abby and Dad and others you've known since high school, but that didn't work out so well. Dad got into trouble and was an FBI informant, Craig is in prison, Buzz disappeared and must be dead, and Abby got in a car accident trying to find me at the store south of Seattle."

She sighs. "You have a point, and that reminds me, we need to go visit Abby. She got hurt in that car accident, going to help you."

I frown. "Well, it's her fault. She shouldn't have been driving fast in the snow." Mom goes stone silent, so I say, "Don't you think?"

"The police are looking into that and accusing her of reckless driving. The people in the other car died in the collision. She feels horrible about it."

A hush falls over the wheelhouse, and Mom wipes tears from her face.

I say, "Sorry about that."

She glances at me, her eyes full of tears. "What's gotten into you? You're acting like a little stinker."

I shrug. "I don't know. I don't feel the same anymore."

"Do you want to see a counsellor?"

My shoulders go rigid. "No, I don't. Let's not talk about this anymore."

Mom hunches over the wheel and blows out a breath. I know I hurt her by snipping at her, but I can't help it. It's like a monster inside me wants to be let out. All I want to do is scream about how I caused my Granddad to take me. It's all my fault, but I can't tell Mom or anyone that.

22

IRENA

I turn the wheel and pull the boat alongside a private dock on Grand Island. Kelly hops off, tying dock lines like a pro. It's a shame she doesn't want to take over my business because she knows boating inside out. She's young, and I hope she'll change her mind. I turn off the engine, remove my life vest and step down on the dock, double-checking the lines. "Looks good."

Kelly beams at me and unsnaps the dog's life vest. He shakes and runs up the dock toward land. She tosses the gear in the boat, and I close the door, glancing up a paved road at Tex's house, the first one on the right. "Here we go."

We stride up the hill and approach a large timbered home with tall windows and vaulted ceilings. A pond glimmers out front, and birds chirp. Air scented with the briny sea drifts past. Happy runs in circles and chases a squirrel before joining us.

My phone dings, and Kelly stiffens as I check it. My ex-husband, Jack, texted, 'Abby is being released from the hospital later today. Can you pick us up and take us home? How's Kelly?'

I whoosh out a breath, feeling torn in many directions, by caring for my daughter, meeting with my new business partner, responding to distress calls for work and being a good friend. I don't have room to do one more thing. But he is Kelly's father, and she's my best friend.

I stop walking and say to Kelly, "Your dad needs help taking Abby home from the hospital."

Kelly's eyebrows rise. "Let's do it. I want to see her."

"I'll tell him we want to but don't know when we'll be back."

I text Jack. 'On Grand Island with Kelly. Not sure when we'll be in town but want to help. More later.'

He texts back seconds later. 'Thought we could depend on you. Guess not.'

I wince, and Kelly asks, "What did Dad say?"

I shrug and tell a little lie. "He's upset about what happened to Abby."

We continue to the house, and Kelly lifts a heavy ring attached to a metal lion's head, knocking on the huge wood front door. A woman in her sixties with shoulder-length blond hair opens the door and flashes a white-toothed smile.

"I'm glad to see you two," she says, gesturing for us to come in. "Thanks for coming, Kelly. It wouldn't be the same without you. Besides, I bet you'll have some good ideas for how to expand your mother's business, since you've been out on the boat with her so often."

I gulp and step inside. I don't want to expand my business. It runs fine as it is. There's only one of me to handle tasks, and we can't add to my overburdened work load.

Chamber music plays in the background. A fire flickers to my left. Wood floors with area rugs make the space look elegant and welcoming, like somewhere I'd like to live.

Kelly opens her arms. "I love it here. Everything is perfect, and it's so peaceful, compared to living in town."

A flash of concern flickers over my face before I plaster on a smile. I'm jealous that my daughter likes this house better than where we live. How ridiculous. I sigh and say, "It is beautiful, isn't it?"

Tex offers us beverages, and Kelly takes lemonade, while I ask for water. Tex sets out a bowl of water for the dog, and he laps it up. We take seats at a long, live-edged wood table, although I'd rather be on the sofa near the blazing fire. Happy turns in a circle by the fire and plops down with a groan.

Tex says, "Let's get started, shall we? Kelly, we welcome any and all comments you'd like to chip in, so don't hold back. Tell us what you think. You know boats and your mother's business better than I do."

Kelly leans forward, arms on the table. "Okay."

I cross my arms. This is my business, but I feel left out and on the side lines, but maybe it is all in my mind. I blow out a breath and let my arms fall to my sides. This isn't a threat to who I am. Tex is trying to help me become more successful. Still, a silent persistent thought pings at the back of my brain. What did I get myself into by taking Tex's money and letting her invest as a business partner?

23

TEX

I sit at the table with Kelly and Irena and sense underlying tension between them. In the past, they laughed and sat leaning toward each other, but now Kelly has a rigid spine, and she doesn't turn to look at her mother when she speaks. Their mouths form thin lines, and they're wired as tight as a taut guitar string.

I tap an index finger on the table. "Who wants to go first with ideas?"

No one speaks. I sigh, recalling a lovely day we had in the past here, where everyone was laughing. Now, in the aftermath of Kelly's kidnapping, we've apparently entered a darker time.

Kelly says, "I wish Mom hadn't taken your money. I know you're nice and you wanted to help my dad when he was in debt, but Mom shouldn't have let anyone else own part of her company."

Irena blinks and stares at her daughter. She reaches out an arm to touch Kelly's shoulder, but Kelly pulls away.

Irena says, "I had no idea you felt that way."

Kelly says in a tear-choked voice, "Well, I'm saying it now. You didn't ask how I felt before."

I nod and realize this is turning into a family therapy session as much as a business meeting, but most small family-owned business discussions with the principals have an emotional component. I hadn't considered that until now. This will be a thorny thicket to cut our way through until we get to business matters and a plan for action, which Irena is clearly resisting, given her body language of crossed arms.

"If you think it would help," I say, "let's get it all out in the open about how and why I became your mom's business partner and a silent investor."

Kelly says, "That's all I wanted to say, for now."

Irena gives me a side glance, so I quickly add, "And I apologize because I'm not silent, am I? I speak up with opinions and enjoy guiding companies to get better results. I think I can help you make a profit on my investment."

Irena nods slowly. "I could use the help. I'm worn out, being pulled in so many directions. Like Jack wants me there at the hospital this afternoon to pick up Abby and take her home. But I can't be everywhere at once. And when distress calls come in, I have to leave Kelly at home or take her with me, which isn't fair to her."

Kelly drums her fingers on the table. "She does that all the time. Even in the middle of dinner, she just up and leaves. I hate it."

"Maybe you need an employee to take calls. Someone to help carry the load."

Irena snorts. "Are you going to come up with magic fairy dust and sprinkle it around? I can't think of anyone I'd trust with my boat, except for Buzz, and he's dead." She and Kelly wipe tears from their eyes.

I sigh. This is going to be more difficult than I anticipated. I stand and say, "How about we take a break for a walk in the woods? When we come back, we'll take a fresh look. I suggest we leave the past behind, right at this table, enjoy the fresh air and come back open to new ideas and being flexible about accepting change."

Kelly and Irena rise. Kelly glances at her mom. "Mom isn't a big fan of change."

Irena chuckles and pats her daughter's shoulder. "You're right. I'm stuck in my habits, and I resist change. But maybe it's time for me to adapt. Let's go."

I glance outside, where dark rain clouds hover over the horizon. I gave Irena a lot of money to get her ex-husband out of debt, and I could walk away from this friction and consider it a wash financially.

Kelly and Irena chat while I grab my coat and smile. These two special people are worth spending my time and effort. Maybe we can find a way for Irena to have more time with Kelly, and for Kelly to get the support she needs. We'll see.

24

———

DUSTY

Zoila pulls me over to a window looking out to her ex-husband's house next door. "Stand here, put your arms around me and kiss me. Make it look good, like you're totally into me."

I step back from her, crossing my arms. "I won't be used to make your ex jealous. He's a nice guy and he's married, so leave him alone."

She frowns and thrusts a hand on her hip. "I bailed you out, so you owe me. You have to do what I say."

I shake my head. "I'm not your puppet, so count me out of your scheme. Do it yourself. I'm heading home to my cabin and staying out of this mess."

"Come on," she says, her beautiful face flushing with frustration. "Help me."

I stride out of her house, letting the storm door slap behind me. "See you later."

She calls in a voice choked with anger, "I won't forget this."

I stride down the block to my truck, which is parked where I left it before Mom's failed home invasion, and hop in. A poem comes to mind, and I say the lines aloud, staring into the dark night.

"Lonely, but surrounded by others.

Escaping clutching arms.

Not a toy to play with.

But a man to be loved, by someone, someday."

I jot down the lines and drive away, releasing a sigh and feeling lucky to have left Zoila behind. She's wily and manipulative, and I'll have to be careful with her.

Tapping on the steering wheel, I review where Mom's home invasion went wrong. My glaring error was underestimating my mother, because she called the cops right away. I thought she'd freak out and wait until it was too late. On the other hand, it worked well to bring the guy from the bar along to shoulder the blame. I'll have to find another way into Mom's house to go on her laptop, get in her bank accounts and transfer money to myself.

Tires whir on the wet road, and I hum to myself. I pass a sign for a campground where my parents took us when we were young, and Dad taught me how to build a fire and chop wood. He made me the man I am today, and I miss him. Tears slide down my cheeks, and I wipe them away.

I go by the place where the sad guy talked about his

dad at a yard sale and where I picked up snowshoes and a motorcycle helmet that came in handy at Mom's. Rubbing my shoulder where Mom hit me with the candlestick, I wince and pull over. Taking a notepad from the glove compartment, I jot down a few lines.

'The best depart first,

Leaving chaff to burn.

Silent warrior, defender, teacher.

Without you, much to learn.'

Storing the notepad in the glove compartment, I light a cigarette and drive away. Making my way in the world is tougher than I thought it'd be without Dad. I need to clear my head and start fresh, given that the anniversary of his death is coming up. A snowshoeing trip by myself in the mountains will do just that, and then I'll know what steps to take next.

I spot a front porch where the homeowners left a bunch of snacks and bottles of water for delivery drivers. I skid to a stop and hop out, leaving the engine running. Hurrying over, I grab as much as my arms will carry and run back to my truck. Laughing as I drive away, I say, "Dinner is served. Thank you, kind people. Appreciate the assist."

25

———————

IRENA

We walk on a dirt trail overlooking the water, and the dog runs through tall grass. Inhaling briny Salish Sea air, I tell myself this is a time to listen and learn. Tex has helped other companies, and she has wisdom to share. Only an idiot would refuse to hear what she has to say.

Kelly smiles. "I wish I could live here. Look, you can see porpoises over there."

I squint and see a pod of porpoises leaping in unison, water shining on their black backs.

Tex chuckles. "Seeing porpoises is said to be a sign of good luck."

I nod. "We could use that, after all that's happened."

Kelly turns and strides ahead, and Tex takes me aside, saying in a low voice, "How's she doing? I've been worried about her."

"It's been rough, and she's testy at times, but who wouldn't be after her ordeal? I've been trying to get her to go to counselling, but she's refusing, even if I go too. I'm not sure what more I can do."

Tex squeezes my hand. "You're doing a great job. Just keep doing what you're doing."

I swallow a lump in my throat. "Thanks."

Back at Tex's house, we sit down with mugs of tea for Kelly and Tex and a cup of coffee for me. Tex throws out ideas, and I sit on my hands and try not to shoot them down as soon as the words leave her mouth. Sure, I know the boat rescue business, but she knows how to turn profits, so I want to listen to what she has to say.

An hour later, I say, "Thanks for this. I'll mull over your ideas and get back to you. And I'll keep an ear open for someone to hire part-time or full-time. I like your suggestion of raising my rates, since my competitors charge more. I'll do that right away."

Kelly half-smiles at me. "But some of your customers already complain about how much it costs to tow their boats to the marina or patch a hole in their hulls."

I grin. "I can handle it."

Tex beams. "We could try some publicity too, to raise your visibility."

I groan and lean back. "No, thanks. I'll pass on that."

Tex brightens. "You know what would make a really good story that the new outlets would eat up?"

Kelly and I look at each other and shake our heads, mystified.

"A mother and daughter boat rescue business. I can see it now, the headlines, the above the fold stories with photos. That would work."

Kelly tilts her head. "Maybe, if it's what Mom wants."

My chest grows tight, and my hands turn cold. I say, "I'm camera-shy and like to stay in the background."

Tex says, "Then it might be a good time to change that. Pretend you like having your picture taken."

I roll my eyes. "Maybe. But right now we need to head back to town. Jack and Abby need us to pick them up at the hospital. Thanks for your support."

Kelly chimes in as we make our way to the front door. "Yeah, thanks."

We wave goodbye and walk down the road with the dog, and I smile to myself. Maybe this is the day that brings my daughter back from her funk, and she will now be the girl she was, all sunshine and roses.

On the way to the boat, Kelly chatters about how it would be great to live here, away from mean kids at school, and a chill runs up my spine. I've got to find a way to fend off this crazy idea of hers to leave town and escape her problems. I know what it's like to be the odd one out in school, and if I could survive my childhood, she can too. We're made of hardy stuff.

26

JACKLYN

I glance at an email from the city and frown at their requirement for an environmental survey before they'll approve my building permit for a subdivision overlooking town. I go online, research companies and call three. One is booked six months out. Another doesn't answer the phone. By the time I dial the third number, I'm ready to be done with this unpleasant task that calls for money coming from my pocket.

A woman says in a warm voice, "Hello, Prospect Services."

"I need an environmental survey for my property. Do you conduct those?"

"Yes, but I'm in the middle of something. Can I call you back?"

"Fine." I give her my number and hang up, thoroughly discouraged. I've got to toughen up or my new business venture will bring me down. To my surprise, five minutes later, the phone rings, and the same woman is on the other end of the line.

She says, "Sorry I had to call you back. Yes, we offer environmental surveys. How can I help you?"

"I own acreage in Millersville and plan to build homes on it, but the City of Millersville is requiring an environmental survey before they'll approve a building permit. How much might that cost and when could we schedule it?"

"I just had a cancellation, so we can get you in three weeks from now. It'll cost three to six thousand dollars, depending on how extensive it is and how large the plot of land."

I put a hand to my forehead and suppress a groan.

She says, "If you don't take that spot, I'll offer it to my other clients, and it'll be a six to ten month wait."

"Okay, please put my name down. Is there any way we can do it earlier?"

"No, I'm afraid not. We're fully booked."

I give her my contact information and hang up. How Dusty did this job is a wonder, with all the details, hounding people, tracking ongoing activities and dealing with bankers. It is so sad that I can't trust my son, and we can't do this together. But I can't trust him, especially after he broke my door down and brought another man to invade my home.

27

IRENA

Kelly and I hop in the boat with the dog and race home from Grand Island to Millersville. Jack texts Kelly and asks if we'll pick them up at the hospital to bring them home.

Kelly says, "Dad's really upset, and it's not good for him after his brain injury. Are we going to pick them up or not?"

"Tell him yes, and we'll be there as soon as we can."

She looks up from her phone. "He's asking for an estimated arrival time."

"My best guess is four."

She types a text. "He says a guess isn't good enough. He needs a definite time. He doesn't want Abby waiting out in the cold."

I stretch my tight shoulders. "Tell him we'll be there by four-thirty."

A log floats ahead in the water, and I pull back on the throttle, slow our speed and steer around the hole-in-the-hull, propeller bending, offending chunk of wood. Seagulls call, water sloshes against the hull, and rain drops splatter the windshield.

I take a deep breath of salty sea air and turn to Kelly, who is sitting still, listening to the water world surrounding us.

I say, "Pretty amazing, isn't it?"

"I can see why you love it. Now let's go get Dad and Abby."

Pushing on the throttle, I steer around the log and take off for the marina. We dock and hop in the car, pulling up at the hospital, where Abby is in a wheelchair waiting outside. Jack uses a cane to walk, and the bandage around his head is gone. In its place are tufts of baby hair growing in where they shaved his skull before an operation.

Kelly leaps out of my car when I stop and runs into his arms. He hugs her and says, "Can you help Abby into the car?"

I climb out and move the front passenger seat back before helping my friend, who is married to my ex-husband, which is weirder than words, into my car. She groans as she settles in the front passenger seat. Jack and Kelly climb in the back with the dog, who licks their faces. An aide takes the wheelchair into the hospital, and I drive slowly away.

Going over a speed bump, Abby moans.

I glance over to her. "Sorry to see you like this."

She chuckles. "You and me both."

Kelly says, "I can't wait until I can drive."

Abby and I look at each, eyebrows raised. "Not so fast, grasshopper," I say, "There's no rush, just a couple of years to go."

Kelly makes a face in the back seat, and Abby says quietly, "I swear, the accident wasn't my fault. The road was slick, and the car in front of me stopped all of a sudden to avoid hitting a deer crossing the freeway, but I didn't see it. It hurts so much, and I feel so sorry for them and their families."

A hush falls over the car as we all ruminate about death and the loss of loved ones. We drop Abby and Jack off at their house and promise to bring their dog over soon, even though they can't walk him, for a visit.

At home, Kelly walks the dog, leading him away from the house with a brisk stride. When she comes back, rosy-cheeked and smiling, she says, "I'm spending the night at Plum's."

"I was hoping we could hang out and watch a movie."

She grabs her backpack and strides out the door. "We can do it another night. See you later."

"Wait," I call from the front door into the drizzling rain to my black hoodie-clad daughter. "When will you be home?"

"Tomorrow sometime. See you later. Love you, Mom."

She runs down the street and disappears around a

corner. I bend and pet the dog, shaking my head at how our easy-going relationship has unraveled. Whatever we were before she was taken has come undone, and she's growing older. She's becoming her own person as a teenager. With a sigh, I check my phone for Kelly's location and nod. She's on her way to her friend's house, just like she said, so I don't have to worry.

My phone rings with a call from a frantic boater who needs help. When I tell them my new, higher rate, they don't balk. I say, "I'll be there as soon as I can."

I hang up, pull on a jacket, grab my purse and race out of the house, ready to rescue another boater in distress.

28

JACKLYN

I drum my fingers on the steering wheel and drive to meet my banker. Walking in the bank, I'm directed to a small office, where I sit and wait. A clock on the wall ticks, reminding me that with each passing minute, I'm losing valuable time moving my project ahead. I've got to get close to breaking ground on Stone Estates or my potential local investors will back out.

The commercial banker glides down the hall and closes the door. She shakes my hand with a firm grip and gestures to a visitor's chair. I take a seat, and she sits, adjusting her gray skirted two-piece suit. She says, "Let's get right down to it. I've looked over your financial statement, and I'll be honest with you. There are many risky projects out there now, given the economic uncertainty, and I thought yours might be one of them."

I hold my breath and wait for what she'll say next. I'm afraid if I speak, I'll say the wrong thing and jinx it.

"But upon further evaluation, it looks to us like your project might be just what we're looking for. You have good credit, you know how to run a business, given your garden store experience, and we like the idea of an upscale housing development with water views near town. This could pencil out very nicely, so we're offering you a commercial loan."

I lean forward and nod. "I'm glad to hear that. What are the terms?"

She taps a pen on her desk blotter. "A five-year commercial loan at ten percent interest."

My mouth hangs open. I manage to say in a tight voice, "Ten percent?"

She nods, unaffected by my panic. "Yes, and you're lucky to get a loan at all, given our rigorous review process."

"But what happens after five years? I won't be able to pay it off then."

"You'll apply to refinance, but I can't guarantee you'll be approved for a new loan, and it could possibly be at higher interest rates."

I gulp, questioning why I thought this project was such a good idea to pursue. I was forced to exit my garden store business when Dusty sold my shop while I was locked away at Shore Lodge. Maybe I have lost my sanity, as he keeps saying, because after that, I dove into the deep end of risk and decided to build a subdivision, about which I know next to nothing about, except for what I overheard my son and husband yammer on about for many years.

I rise. "Thank you. I'll have to think it over."

She walks me to the door of her office. "Don't wait too long. Rates are going up every day. You'll need to move ahead on this in the next few days, or the loan offer won't be valid. Oh, by the way, it's a secured loan."

I cock my head. "Secured against what? My savings?"

She shakes her head. "The loan will be secured against your house as collateral."

I close my open mouth and thank her, hustling out the door and thoroughly mortified at the high costs involved in construction. The amount of risk involved makes my armpits prickle with sweat. This building project will require big bucks, a tough backside and a truckload of determination.

I climb in my car, slam the door shut and vow to prove to my son wrong. I know I have the smarts, mettle and moxie to pull this off.

29

KIRK'S WIFE

My husband gets out of bed and shuffles to the bathroom, quietly closing the door. He thinks I can't hear him, and although he turned on the faucet, I hear him talking on the phone with someone. I grit my teeth and throw on a pair of sweatpants and a matching blue sweatshirt. I bet he's talking in whispered tones to Zoila, his former wife, who he conveniently moved in right next door.

Slamming the bedroom door behind me, I stomp down to the kitchen and brew a pot of coffee the way I like it, even though I know he'll hate it. But he deserves a bitter brew after installing what I suspect is his mistress next door.

I swallow and listen to the coffee pot burble, hiss and perk. He's keeping secrets, and I know it. We were happy and contented before Zoila wiggled her way into our lives, shimmying around in skimpy clothes, standing too close to my husband and hugging him for way too long. The other day, I caught Kirk watching her from our bedroom window. She was undressing in front of her window. How crazy is that?

When I saw him gaping at her, I dropped the coffee cup I was carrying, and he jumped in the air. I didn't bother to clean it up. I shot him a cold stare and strode away, closing the bathroom door, leaning against the sink and wondering how our relationship had gotten to this point. He knocked and asked to come in, but I said, "Not now."

Since then, he's been on the phone, talking to her in hushed, urgent tones, and hurrying over there when he thinks I'm not watching, or I'm supposed to be running errands. I've heard him tiptoe out the door and walk, looking over his shoulder, next door, where she gives him a hug and ushers him inside.

Now, in the kitchen, I pour a hot steaming mug of coffee and sit at the breakfast bar, drumming my fingers on a cold granite slab. He's been responding to her every plea for help. Is she really sick, or is she faking it to get his attention?

I frown, recalling how on a recent evening, he left his dinner cooling on a plate and hurried over there to fix her running toilet, She's a siren, luring him in, and I'll do whatever it takes to protect our marriage and send her packing.

30

───────

KELLY

Light rain patters as I head to my friend's house. Ahead, Vista and Avery stand under an awning outside a corner store. I give them a little wave and hope I don't look as awkward as I feel. I don't know them, but as class outcasts, we have much in common.

"Hey, Kelly," Avery says, tugging on a strand of her hair.

Vista eyes me. "Where are you going?"

I shrug. "To spend the night at Plum's. Maybe make some gluten-free cookies."

Avery steps toward me, and my pulse picks up. There's something dangerous about these two, although they're my age. "Why don't you hang with us instead?"

Vista grins. "Yeah, stash your stuff at Plum's and leave your phone there, so your mom can't track you. We'll show you what we do at night, when the wolves are out."

My heart thunders in my chest. I know I shouldn't join them, because my mom wouldn't like it. She stays the steady course and is rule bound. But after that I went through, I want a bigger life, with more color and risk. "Sure."

Avery says in a low voice, "Yeah, stash your backpack and come back, and we'll tell you what we're doing. But you have to promise not to tell anyone, not even Plum. She'd rat us out and get us in trouble."

Vista nods.

I take a deep breath. My hands grow cold. I feel like I'm on the edge of a cliff, looking down and about to leap. "Sure, okay. I'll be back. Just got to stow this stuff."

Vista says, "You should be all right if you put it under their front steps or the deck. But it's important to leave your phone, so they can't track you."

"Got it." I stride away on shaking legs and make my way to Plum's. I didn't tell her I was coming over, so she won't wonder where I am when I don't show up. Unzipping the backpack, I pull out the whip my grandfather had that I kept when I was abducted. I stuff it in my waistband, hide the backpack under Plum's front porch and run back to the street corner. This feels dangerous and exciting, and I hope I'll find peace with the person I've become.

31

IRENA

Hopping in my boat, my pulse pounds, and I warm up the engine. I putter slowly through the marina, so as not to leave a wake. Out in the bay, I push on the throttle and the boat flies across waves. Rain drums down on the wheelhouse, windshield wiper blades swish back and forth, and I hunch over the wheel, heading for Watmough Bay.

My phone rings, and I answer it. My ex-husband, Jack, says, 'We need groceries. Can you bring milk, eggs and bread for us?"

I sigh and turn south in Rosario Strait, keeping a sharp eye out for Washington State ferry boats, tug boats pulling barges, pleasure boats and tankers. On any given day, the wide body of water can be populated by many types of water craft, each going in a different direction with a set purpose, and not necessarily keeping an eye out for other marine traffic. To assume is deadly in the Salish Sea.

"I wish I could, but I'm out on a call. I don't know when I'll be back in town."

"What'll we do?" he says in a whining tone. "We're stuck in our house, and neither of us can drive."

Blowing out a breath, I tell myself I don't have to rescue my ex from his fate. He got himself in debt, was pursued by a thug and was involved in a scam, turning into an FBI informant. I say, "This isn't forever, you know. You'll be able to walk again fine, maybe in a few months. And Abby's broken bones will heal."

"You're not a doctor. You don't know."

I roll my eyes. This is why he is my ex-husband, and now he's Abby's problem. "Call an Uber."

"I don't know how."

"Abby's smart, ask her to show you."

He whispers, "I don't know how to use a smart phone, and I'm embarrassed. It makes me feel stupid, and my head still hurts."

"Oh Jack, that's awful, but Abby can teach you." I wince at blue tanker bearing down, coming from the south. "Sorry, but I've got to go. Danger approaches."

"Wait, I want to talk about Kelly."

I hang up and turn the wheel, leaving the tanker and the shipping channel behind. Slowing my speed, my boat glides into Watmough Bay, where green water beckons, and seaweed covers ottoman-shaped rocks exposed by low tide.

I sniff the salty sea air and smile. This is my calling. Tall trees on bluffs surround the bay, forming a cathedral of branches reaching to the gray sky. I blink and bring myself back to my work.

Picking up my phone, I dial the boater, and he answers on the first ring. "We're the white-hulled sailboat closest to shore. It's getting shallow, but our anchor won't budge. Can you help us?"

"I'm coming your way. I'll be there in a flash."

I pull up on his starboard side, away from shore, where a wide beach waits for children with sand pails, or hikers to stride across. Tying up to a cleat on his boat, I knock on the hull of his boat. "Permission to come aboard?"

An older gray-haired man appears. His weathered face is drawn. He opens his arms. "Please, come aboard. I came out for the night, but the anchor got stuck. I'm getting really worried."

I nod. "I can see why. With the tide going out, you could be beached here, with the boat lying on its side. We don't have much time, so I'll get in my gear and go see what the problem is. Stand on the bow and be ready to haul up the anchor when I tell you."

When he nods, I say, "But first, I'll need your credit card for a deposit."

His jaw drops. "Now? With all this going on?"

I shrug. "Won't take but a minute. Part of doing business."

"What's your going rate? I'm not sure I want to pay it."

I name an amount, with my new higher rate, and he crosses his arms. "Sounds like highway robbery."

"You're welcome to fix it yourself. Have a good day."

I turn, preparing to board my boat, but he says, "Wait, don't go. I'll pay. I need your help." He holds out a credit card.

Pulling out my phone, I tap his credit card on the app and hand it back to him. "There, that's out of the way. I'll get this fixed for you. Be right back."

I pull on my wet suit and mask, put a sharp knife in my teeth and step off my boat into the frigid water. Strands of seaweed float by as I swim to his anchor. A rope attached to an abandoned anchor is wrapped around my boater's anchor. Taking the knife from my mouth, I cut the line and swim to the surface.

I climb on my boat, pull off my gear, stow the knife, and hurry over to the waiting skipper. The beach behind him looms ever closer. I say, "Go ahead and see if you can pull up your anchor. I'll wait to be sure you're all set."

He hustles to the helm and the winch whines, as his muddy anchor chain slowly comes up, rattling and clanking. He goes to his bow and waves to me. "Thanks."

"Glad to help. I'll release my line and be off."

I cast off from his sailboat and turn away, puttering out of the peaceful bay with a smile on my face. The crack of a gunshot rings out, making me flinch, and a hunter in an orange vest appears in the forest. I guess even in paradise, there are downsides. Nothing is as good as it looks, and there's a hidden price to pay.

I text Jack. 'Free now. Can pick up your groceries. Give me a list.'

He replies. 'No need. Took care of it without you. Call me about Kelly.'

I swallow hard and call Jack. When he picks up, I say, "I'm a little worried about Kelly. She's not acting like herself."

He clears his throat. "I can see why, after what she's been through. Maybe she needs a change of scenery, like living with us, instead of with you."

I gasp, clapping a hand to my chest. "No way. I'm her mother."

"It might not be about what you want, but it's what's best for her. We'll talk more about this later. Abby's calling for me."

He hangs up, and I stare at my phone. There's no way those two could take care of my daughter, not when they're both recovering from injuries. They can't even take care of a dog right now.

I grit my teeth and push on the throttle, flying over waves. Rain splatters the windshield, and I let out a warrior cry. "Kelly, come back to me. I love you. I want to help you."

But the wailing wind is my only reply.

32

KIRK'S WIFE

I 've taken to lurking about and watching what my husband and Zoila next door are doing. I shake my head at how demented I must look, tiptoeing to windows, looking out and wondering if I've lost Kirk to Zoila's clutches. How did we let one person upend our perfect lives?

I grab my purse and call out to Kirk, who is working in his study, "I'm going to the grocery store." When I don't get an answer, I step lightly to his study and crack open the door. He's hunched over his computer, tapping on the keyboard.

I come up behind him and see he's on a bank website, but we don't have an account with them. Patting his shoulder, I say, "What're you doing?'

He flinches, his arms jerk, and he clicks the website closed in the blink of an eye. The laptop screen goes dark.

Swiveling his chair to face me, his brow is beaded with sweat. "You almost gave me a heart attack. Don't surprise me and come in like that."

I tilt my head. "What's going on? Why did you shut down your computer so fast? This isn't like you. And what was that bank account? We don't have money there."

His cheeks flush, and he shrugs. "Nothing. It's got to do with work."

I resist the urge to get angry about his evasiveness. He's hiding something, but it won't help if I push him away into her boa constrictor arms. I must be calm and keep the long game in mind. We were great as a couple, laughing and listening, going out to dinners. until Zoila shimmied her way into our lives, dividing us by her presence.

"Want to go out for coffee?" I say, hoping a change of scenery and distance from the woman next door will heal what is broken.

He averts his eyes and studies the floor. "I'll pass. Got some work to do. Good idea, though. Maybe next time."

He swivels his chair away from me, ending the conversation and shutting me out. He flips through papers on his desk and pretends to be busy, although he's not fooling anyone but himself.

His spurning my offer for a fun outing unleashes an angry beast inside me, and I say in a bitter voice, "I won't wait around forever, while you fool around with herself next door." I wait and tap a toe, but he doesn't respond. His jaw tenses, and his back tightens.

I cross my arms. "I see what's going on under my nose, you know, and how you watch her, and how she hugs you for far too long. You'd better break this off."

He says in a tight voice, "It would be best if you leave me be. I'll be finished in a few hours."

Gritting my teeth, I turn and march out of the room. A thought occurs to me as I cross over the threshold and slam the back door behind me. If it is work-related, he would be right not to share details with me. Maybe I'm imagining what's going on, and I'm overreacting. But who am I kidding?

Stepping into the rain, I walk to my car.

"Hello," someone calls.

I glance over at Zoila, who is leaving her house and waving to me. She says, "I was just coming over to have a cup of coffee with you and Kirk. He texted and invited me. Aren't you joining us?"

I stop and stare at her flimsy floral dress. Rain dampens her hair and face, making her more beautiful, while I feel like a drab, drowned rat. Shaking my head, I say, "No, I'll leave you to it. I'm headed to the grocery store."

She wiggles her fingers. "Bye. See you later."

I get in my car and close the door, leaning back and hoping I won't see her later or ever. She is a thorn in my side, popping by to see Kirk at all hours. And he's part of the problem too, inviting her over.

I start the car and back up. Zoila is knocking on our front door and ringing the bell as if her life depends on it, but Kirk isn't appearing or answering the door. Maybe she is manipulating both of us, and he didn't really invite her over.

Despite the cool weather, I turn on the fan in the car, blasting cold air in my face to clear my head. Something suspicious is going on in my house, and I don't think it's all due to Zoila and her charms.

33

JACKLYN

I call a friend and fellow business owner who was interested in investing in my subdivision and suggest we meet. "Sure," Bernice says. "Come to my office, and we'll talk about it." I park outside her escrow company and walk in, recalling the day I came here and stopped Dusty from selling my house out from under me.

Bernice pops out of her office and comes over, giving me a hug. "Great to see you. Like a cup of coffee?"

The coffee in her office is weak, but I could use a boost of caffeine after being scrutinized by the banker. "Sure. I just came from the bank. Every fiber in my body is weak from the encounter. It was like being examined under a microscope."

She chuckles. "They do look hard before approving a loan. What did you learn?"

She hands me a mug of black coffee, and we walk into

her office, where I settle on the edge of an office chair, clutching a cup in my hands. "My nerves are frayed and frazzled, but they did offer me a construction loan. The problem is, it comes with a high interest rate, which will cut into my profits."

She sets her cup down on her desk. "You're right, carrying costs cut into your profits. Most builders take out home equity loans, instead of commercial loans, because the rates are lower. Why don't you do that?"

"I could, but that amount would be a drop in the bucket, compared to the pool of money I need to build Stone Estates. It's going to be expensive."

Bernice runs a hand through her short gray hair and leans back. "The big dogs tap their home equity and, if they have to, get a loan on top of that." She holds up an index finger. "But first, they line up investors for the project. How's that going for you?"

I smile and hope she'll keep her word and invest in my subdivision. "That's why I came to see you. Are you still interested in backing the project? I hope so."

She cocks her head. "Tell me what's going on with your permit. Do you have it in hand?"

I let out a sigh. "Unfortunately, the permit is stalled for a few months or more. They're requiring an environmental survey. Someone told the planning office there was a wet land adjacent to the parcel and an eagle's nest on the property. I bet I can guess who that person was, and his name is Dusty."

She nods. "He wants his construction company back, with a vengeance. But it might not be bad to get an environmental survey before you build. That way, you can wave it in his face when nothing turns up. And, when you start a project like this, surprises always pop up."

I grimace. "And one six-foot-two surprise happens to be named Dusty Stone."

She stands and says, "I'd better get back to it. We've got three houses to close on this afternoon. It's a tornado of energy around here. Thanks for stopping in."

I rise and my hands tremble, cradling the empty coffee mug. "Can I count you in for the project?"

She averts her eyes. "Let me think about it. The delay in timing throws a wrench in the works, I have a conflict. I promised to help my brother buy a house, and family comes first. I'm sure you understand."

My stomach sours, and I force a smile. "I do."

I leave the mug in the kitchen area, say goodbye with a heavy heart and walk to my car. Sliding in the driver's seat, I start the car and mutter to myself, "I hope I'm not over my head, and I've got to figure this out."

34

KELLY

Vista hands me a black sweatshirt at a park. "Put this on and pull up the hood, so no one will see your face." I do what she says, ignoring a small voice inside warning me Mom would freak out if she knew I wasn't at Plum's, where I said I'd be.

Avery hands me a small plastic bottle filled with amber-colored liquid. "Drink this."

Taking a big swig and acting tough, I gasp and cough, clawing at the air at the awful taste. I hand the bottle back to her. "What is it?"

"Booze I stole from my dad. He buys these at the liquor store and chugs them down on family picnics when he pretends to take phone calls and walks off. He thinks I don't notice, but I do."

My throat burns, and I swallow to get rid of the bitter taste. "Why would anyone drink that stuff?"

She grins. "To feel happy, like this."

Avery and Vista run around, laughing and shrieking at the top of their lungs. My stomach doesn't feel right, and I wince, my eyes darting around, and sit down. I hope my mom's friends won't spot us and call her to report what I'm doing, but I know in a small town like ours, you can't hide for long before someone finds out your secrets.

Watching cars pass, I feel light-headed and frown. Granddad broke the bubble of my small world when he took me, and since that afternoon, I've been in a dark place. I want to numb myself to the pain of recurring angry thoughts that hammer away relentlessly in my mind. I stand and wipe my hands on my jeans.

"Come on," Avery calls.

I twirl around and yell for joy, even though it feels forced and fake, until I flop on the ground with the sky above me whirling around. Life can't go back to the way it was before I was kidnapped, but maybe these new friends will support me on my journey.

I sit up, and Avery plops down next to me. She leans over and says with boozy breath, "You should see what we do at night. It's so much fun. You won't believe it."

We run around for a few hours, and my stomach growls. I say, "I'm hungry. Where can we get food?"

They laugh and traipse into the nearby corner store. Avery says, "Dad, can we have some food?"

A middle-aged man with curly brown hair grins. "Take whatever you like, ladies."

We heat bean burritos in a microwave and run into the park, sitting at a picnic table. I take a bite, burn the roof of my mouth and let out a yelp. Dropping the burrito on the foil wrapper, I wince and wish I was at Plum's place or with my mom, eating home cooked food with people I know well. I squirm on the hard seat and nibble at the food, listening to the other two chatter.

When darkness settles in for the night, I shiver and cross my arms for warmth, letting out a huge yawn. My butt is cold from sitting on a park bench. It would be much more comfortable at home.

"It's time," Vista says, pointing out of the park.

I blink and tell myself to wake up. "Time for what?"

She smiles. "What we do at night. We run in the road. Come on, it's fun."

She holds out a hand, and I take it, hauling myself up and standing on trembling legs like a newborn fawn taking its first steps. I hope I'm doing the right thing by hanging out with them. I swallow as my mother's voice rings in my ears. 'Be safe.' But it's too late for that.

Vista and Avery take me to meet a group of kids. The leader is Erlene, and she points to a black tarmac road cloaked in darkness. "Let's scare drivers tonight and run out in the road, pounding on their windows. It'll freak them out. They'll piss in their pants."

I cock my head. "Why do you do that?"

Erlene studies me. "You'll find out. It'll make you feel alive."

I raise my eyebrows and chew on my lower lip. They stare at me, as if waiting for a response, and I say, "I'm not sure about this. It sounds dangerous, and I don't want to get hurt. I don't want to add to my mom's worries. She needs me."

Vista slaps my shoulder. "Come on, don't back out now. It'll be great."

Under her breath, Erlene says, "Chicken."

Avery says with a smile, "You'll like it once you try it."

I shrug and decide to give it a chance. "Okay, fine. Show me what to do."

At two in the morning, I join others darting in and out of traffic, running between cars on Highway 20 as they slow down coming into town. A car skids to a stop, and the driver rolls down her window, yelling, "You should be home in bed. Where are your parents? Someone should be watching you."

I run away giggling, and the car drives off. With my hands on my knees, I'm panting and short of breath, but every nerve in my body is alive. I grin and pull Granddad's whip out of my waistband. Running out in the road, I crack the whip at a car, and a man shakes a fist. Another driver floors it, hightailing it into town.

Vista says. "What are you doing with a whip? Where did you get that?"

"My granddad gave it to me."

"Wow, way cool. Wish I had one like that."

Wanting her to like me, I hand it to her. "You can borrow it."

Vista runs away laughing and snapping the whip at passing cars. A squad car pulls up with flashing lights, and I hide in the bushes. An officer takes the whip from her and ushers her into the back of his squad car, telling her he'll take her home. She shouldn't be out this late at thirteen. She should know better.

I stand there watching, tears wetting my cheeks. I lost my whip and a new friend tonight. That whip represented power and the ability to control people who have gone astray. I bet I can get another one from a costume shop, but it won't be the same as the one I grabbed from my grandfather after he whipped me.

I stand by the side of the road while Avery and others run out, pounding on car windows and darting through cars to get to the other side. Standing there, I realize I've already been to the other side, and I don't need to run across in the dark and endanger my life. I've been through that already with Granddad, so why would I risk my life again?

Avery runs over. "Isn't this fun?"

"Not so much," I say, frowning.

She links her arm in mine. "Let's go to my house. You can sleep there."

"Okay, I guess. I was thinking of going home, but my mom would have a fit."

"Stay with me. Come on. You can go home tomorrow."

35

———

IRENA

I climb out of bed in the morning, stretch my arms and realize I haven't heard from Kelly. A flicker of doubt flits through my mind, and I wonder if she is at Plum's, like she said. I march to her closed bedroom door and it dawns on me that I'm being overly anxious. She said she'd be home this morning, and it's only nine o'clock.

I knock lightly and get no answer, so I knock a second time and then crack open the door. Kelly's room smells like sweet girl-sweat, old sneakers and jeans that could use a good spin in the washing machine.

A lump in bed draws me closer. I bend and pat the lump, where Kelly's shoulders should be, but it's soft and formless. She's not here. She's at her friend's house.

Sea air blows in through the open window. I sit on the edge of the bed massaging my temples. Talking about overreacting over nothing. Kelly is staying at Plum's, so I shouldn't be worried. I grab my phone to check Kelly's location, and it shows her phone at her friend's house.

Just to be sure, I text Plum's mom. 'Thanks for having Kelly last night, Hope she wasn't much trouble. What time should I pick her up?"

Plum's mom texts, 'Kelly isn't here. We haven't seen her in a few days.'

My body turns cold, and a chill runs up my spine. My daughter deceived me. If she isn't there, where is she?

36

ZOILA

When Jacklyn drives away from her house, I text Dusty with an update, because he's supposedly paying me to watch his mom and report on her activities. A strange man with a red polka dot bow tie clipped to his long gray beard enters Jacklyn's house, so I text Dusty about that. He replies, 'Keep the information coming. Good work.'

I hurry next door to see my ex-husband and run into Kirk's new wife. When I say the three of us were supposed to meet for coffee at their place, she grows cold and leaves to get groceries.

I arrange my hair the way Kirk likes, hanging down in front of my shoulders, and knock. No one answers, but I ring the bell a few times, and Kirk finally comes to the door. From the dark circles under his eyes, he looks like he hasn't had much sleep lately, and he won't meet my eyes.

I smile and let my long blue velvet cape fall open. He never could resist a flimsy white lacy negligee when we were married. "Aren't you going to invite me in? We're safe until your new wife comes back."

He stays inside and locks the storm door. "We can't do this anymore. I don't want her to find out."

Tilting my head, I plaster on my most ingratiating smile. "Come on, let me in."

He waves his hands, behind the storm door. "No, I can't. I'm done with whatever this is."

I put my hands on my hips. "Kirk, are you listening to me?" I say in my most seductive voice, "Let me in. Your wife will never know what we're up to."

He moans, running a hand through his thinning hair. Unlocking the door, he opens it. Motioning me inside, he says, "Quick, before someone sees us."

37

DUSTY

I'm hanging out in my cabin when thirst calls, and I grab a beer for breakfast from the refrigerator. The can is cold in my hands, and I stop to look out the window while I pop the top, staring at Mount Skuksan towering above. I could start a mountain trekking company and take people on tours, snowshoeing through deep, crisp snow. Winter sun shines, making snow on the ground sparkle, and I nod. All it would take would be a few posters on bulletin boards, and my new business would be hopping in no time.

Clomping around the cabin, I guzzle beer, throw it in the sink and sniff musty air, glancing at the snowshoes I recently acquired. The guy with the yard sale mentioned warming temperatures, but I'm athletic and nimble. How hard could it be to venture out in the mountains in this weather? I'm not going overnight or anything. It'll be a piece of cake.

I pick up the snowshoes and load my backpack with a bottle of water and a granola bar. I won't be out for long, and this will clear my head. The home invasion at Mom's didn't go as planned, and no one at the bar in Foothills will speak to me, so I might as well take this hike.

Whistling a tune, I grab my backpack and head out. Things are going to go my way from now on. I can just feel it.

38

JACKLYN

I park in my garage and stride to the house, eager to see Buddy and Mercury. Two raccoons in my yard watch me from ten feet away and sit up on their back feet, holding out their paws. I shake my head. "You're cute, but we've got nothing for you." They come closer, and I wave my hands. "Go away, shoo! And stay away from my dog."

Tromping in my house, I close the door and lean back against it, letting out a long sigh. I glance out the front window, where three raccoons are watching the house. I shake my head, and pat Buddy, who is whining at the window. "They'll soon outnumber us."

"Hey, you're back. We missed you," Mercury says, sitting on the sofa.

I slump into an arm chair and groan.

Buddy hops up next to him, and he pats Buddy's back. "That bad, huh?"

I open my hands. "I can't believe it. Bernice turned me down. She was going to be my big investor for the building project. I don't know what to do."

"You'll think of something." He pets my dog's head. "Isn't that right, Buddy? You know her best."

I roll my eyes, but at the same time, I appreciate the support. "I need to come up with a solution."

"Up a creek without a paddle, huh?"

I nod. "I am. What would you suggest? Bernice said I should refinance my house, but it wouldn't bring in near enough money to build those high-end homes."

He adjusts his bow tie. "Have you considered dropping the project entirely and selling the land? It'd be less stress for you. I hate to see you upset like this."

I give him the stink eye. "I hope you're pulling my leg, because I'm not giving this up. It was my husband's dream, and I feel an obligation to see this through."

"But is it your dream, as well as his and your son's? Are you only doing this because you feel obligated? No one is making you do this, from what I can see."

I make a face. "I want to do it and feel I ought to make the effort to complete this plan. I lost my garden store because of what Dusty did, but I should be able to learn a new set of skills and offer people beautiful homes."

He shrugs. "Give it time. Maybe there are other solutions you haven't thought of yet."

"I'm going to go out and work in the yard and breathe fresh air."

He glances outside, raising his eyebrows. "Now? When it's raining?"

I stand. "Of course. Why not?"

"Because it's wet and cold and winter is why."

I smile and get my coat. "That's never stopped me before. Come on, Buddy, we're going outside." Buddy hops down from the couch and shakes, but I stop at the door. "I'm sorry, Buddy, I forgot about the raccoons. I think it's too dangerous for you."

I pick up an air horn I used on boats and slip outside, closing the door behind me. I hope inhaling the salt air will clear my mind of troubles. Four raccoons gather in my front yard and stare at me. When I honk the horn, they climb the fence and head to Zoila's.

Working with dirt will free up fresh ideas for how to attract money for my project. I don't feel right asking friends for money, especially not Abby who was just hurt in a car crash. I don't want to beg like a raccoon for handouts, but I've got to figure this mess out.

The front door opens, and Mercury comes out, pulling his hood up over his hat. "I'll give you a hand, although it's crazy to be outside on a day like this. Okay if I let Buddy out in the yard?"

Surveying the property and seeing no raccoons, I say, "Sure, they went away. He should be safe as long as he stays in the fenced yard."

39

DUSTY

I whistle at the trailhead and strap on snowshoes, heading into the woods. The going is tough through wet, deep snow, but I make headway up the mountain. After this outing, I'll head back and find a bar and grab a beer. Maybe I'll find someone to buy me beers, and they'll become a new friend.

Seven miles in, a man with a flushed face trudges toward me. He stops, wiping beads of sweat from his brow. "Don't go out there today. It's perfect conditions for an avalanche. We've got warming temperatures."

My hands clench. I hate it when people tell me what to do. "I can handle it."

He cocks his head, eying the mountain. "If an avalanche races down, there's nowhere to hide. You have to respect the mountain, be prepared and, whatever you do, don't cross the snow field straight ahead."

I glare at him. "I know what I'm doing."

"Do you have a beacon to set off, so rescuers can locate you under the snow?"

I shrug. "Nope, I don't need high-tech stuff. I'm an old school kind of guy."

The man glances at the mountain and the warm shining sun. He scratches his salt and pepper beard and opens his pack, pulling out a device shaped like a cell phone.

Clicking a button, he hands it to me. "My buddy gave me this extra avalanche transceiver, so you might as well have it. Wear it close to your body, and if you hear the crack of the avalanche, run for cover and set off the beacon."

"That's nice of you, but I doubt I'll need it." I try to hand it back to him, but he waves my hand away.

"Keep it and don't stay out long. It's dangerous. I'm on the search and rescue team and hope we won't get called to come back here and dig you out."

I wave as he leaves. "See you around."

He heads toward the parking lot, and when his back is turned, I give him the middle finger. What a jerk. I hate people who think they know it all.

A soft breeze carries a hint of warm air, and I shake my head. That guy was way too worried about conditions on the mountain. Nothing bad will happen today in this pristine wilderness. The mountain is my friend, not an enemy to be feared.

I lift my snowshoed feet and set them down, thighs burning from the effort. Glistening white snow crunches with each step. All is quiet, with no one else around.

Breathing hard, I stop to take in the beauty and study the wide-open snow field ahead. I look up at the craggy tall towering mountain and inhale crisp, cool air. Trudging ahead to get a better view, lines of a poem run through my mind, and I say the words out loud as I slog ahead.

"There is enough love.

There is enough time.

There is a beginning and an end.

We are one with all that is."

I continue on, drawn by the still silence of the pristine wilderness. A hush falls over the mountain. I stop midway through the snowfield and gape at the snow-covered mountain looming above.

A sense of something about to happen tickles at the back of my neck, but I brush it away. That search and rescue guy was all worry and no fun. I know what I'm doing.

40

KELLY

The sound of heavy footsteps wakes me, and a man stumbles down a hall, swearing. My eyes dart around. My hands clench, and my pulse picks up. I don't know where I am. I sit up from sleeping on the floor with a blanket over me and look around a tiny room with one small, smudged window. A narrow bed is empty, with covers tossed aside.

I put a hand to my aching forehead and remember what I did last night. Swallowing bitter bile, my stomach heaves, and I throw open the door, searching for the bathroom.

The door to what might be a bathroom down a dim hall is locked. "Busy," a man says in a low voice. I cringe and pull my hand away, racing for the front door, where I puke my guts out on a bush by the entry.

Avery comes up the front walkway with a newspaper

in her hands. She grins. "I took it from the neighbors. They'll never miss it."

My stomach churns, and I tell my roiling gut to settle down. I swear, after this, I'll never drink alcohol again, not ever in my life. I bend over and a rush of vomit spills out of my mouth.

Avery wrinkles her nose. "Gross, couldn't you puke away from the house? That's what I do. I run around back and barf in the bushes where no one sees it."

I cross my arms, and rain drizzles down on my head.

She says, "We should stay out here for a while. My dad's in the bathroom and it'll stink up the house."

I wince and have a sudden urge to go home and be with my mother. I don't belong here. I want to be home. "How far is it to Plum's from here, do you think? A mile?"

She points to my mouth. "You have a little throw up on your lips."

I cringe and wipe my mouth with the back of my hand. I can't wait to get out of here and be home, where everything is familiar and comfortable without stinky smells.

She says, "Yeah, Plum's place is about a mile. She and I used to be friends, but she didn't like what I was doing at night. She said it was dangerous, and I might get hit by a car."

I massage my throbbing temples. "Which way do I go? I was so out of it last night, I forget. I have to get my backpack with my phone before I sneak home."

She fixes her eyes on mine, and I get the feeling this is a make-or-break moment in our new friendship. "My dad can drive you there when he gets out of the bathroom, which could be a long time."

My body goes rigid. I don't want to spend more time with her or her father. I don't want to be stuck in a car with a strange man, even if he is her dad. The urge to run makes me hop from one foot to the other. "No thanks, I've got to go. I'll just go get my shoes."

I go in her room and pull on my sneakers, my hands shaking as I tie them. She stands in the doorway watching me, and if I had to guess, she's insulted at how fast I want to flee. I stand and say, "Thanks, I'll see you around."

Her eyebrows arch. "Yeah, see you around, but don't tell anyone what we did."

In a trembling voice, I lie and say, "My lips are sealed. Sorry about the mess I made."

She shrugs. "I'll hose it off. No big deal."

I hurry out the front door. Full of pent-up energy, remorse and self-hatred, I take off running as fast as I can, cutting through a park and leaping over curbs. Swinging my arms and puffing hard, I race to Plum's yard, keeping my head down so they won't see me out the windows. I'll grab my backpack and run home before Mom notices I'm not where I said I'd be. I reach for my backpack, and a woman's voice close by makes me blink and look up.

Plum's mom says, "I saw you through the window and

texted your mother saying you're here. She's worried out of her mind. Where were you?"

I gulp and press my lips together, staying quiet because I only have one mother to answer to. I don't have to tell this kind woman what I was doing. Plum comes out of the house in flannel pajamas. We stand in the rain, a sorry trio, all three of us frowning and silent.

Plum finally says, "I don't understand why you're here, and why you told your mom you were staying over when you weren't."

I open my hands. "I guess I wanted to see what it was like to hang out with other people for once."

She shakes her head and turns to go inside. "We're not friends anymore. You can hang out with anyone you like, but you didn't have to hurt my feelings in the process. You're not who I thought you were."

"Wait, don't go," I say, but she goes inside and closes the door. I make to run after her, but her mother blocks my way. "I'm sorry," I call.

Her mom says in a stern voice, "You should be."

A car screeches to a halt out front, and my mom jumps out, leaving the driver's side door open. She runs over and opens her arms, hugging me until I can't breathe.

Pulling back, she stares at me. "Kelly, I was so worried. What happened and why did you lie to me?"

I mumble, "I'll tell you when we're home."

She guides me to the car and calls to Plum's mom, who

is watching us from the front porch, "Thanks for texting me."

I finch in the passenger seat. "Wait, I forgot my back-pack. I have to go get it."

I make to open the car door, but she puts a hand on my arm, stopping me. "Leave it. We'll come back later for it."

I say in a whining voice, "But it has my homework and my phone. I've got to get it."

"Fine," she says. "I'll get it. You stay here. We have a lot to talk about."

Trembling in the car, I cross my arms and watch Mom pick up my backpack and stride back to the car. Her jaw is set, and she is frowning like I've never seen before.

41

IRENA

I grit my teeth and drive, hunched over the wheel and resisting the urge to turn and glare at my daughter. She says, "I didn't do anything. You shouldn't be mad at me."

I snort. "Save it for someone who'll believe you. We both know what you did was wrong, and you can't convince me otherwise."

She whines, drawing out the word, "Mom," making it into three syllables.

I snap out my next words. "You reek of booze on your breath. Your clothes smell like smoke and vomit. You're wearing someone else's black hoodie. It's hard to listen to you lie and say you didn't do anything. You are grounded for a month, if not more, and I'm taking away your phone."

Kelly gasps. "You can't do that."

I turn the corner and go down our block, clamping my mouth shut. Arguing with a teenager is a fruitless task. I can't believe she's flat out lying to me.

Parking in my driveway, I pull out my key and march toward the house. She follows hot on my heels and says, "Mom, you can't do that. I need my phone. What if something happens, and I need to call you?"

"Oh yes, I can. Someone needs to be the adult around here."

I fling open the front door, and she stalks past me to her room, calling over her shoulder, "Fine, I don't care anyway."

In a loud voice, I say, "I'm coming in your room after we've both cooled off, and I want to hear exactly what you did and who was involved."

She slams the door, and pictures on the wall rattle. We've got our own earthquake here in our house. I sink into a chair and put my head in my hands.

42

DUSTY

Sweat trickles down my arms, and I gaze at the snow-covered mountain. Cold air sweeps off the summit, blowing down, and tears slide down my cheeks, thinking of Dad. The anniversary of his death is coming up, and trekking outside is a fitting way to remember him. We always meant to do this, but he was busy at work and couldn't take time off.

Snow beneath my feet sinks, crunching underfoot. Water drips nearby. The bright sun hovers in a clear, blue sky. I clear my throat and wipe tears away. On a perfect day to be outdoors, and I'm alone, like I've always been,

Something changes in the air, and a shiver runs up my spine. Despite the calm scene of a snow field before me, I sense tension building. I rub my arms, where hairs stand on end.

I tilt my head, straining to hear a subtle sound

growing louder. The air sharpens around me. A rock rolls down the mountain, gathering speed as it heads toward me.

Hearing a low rumble, every fiber of my being tells me to run. The mountain trembles under my feet. I lift my legs and hurry toward safety, but fall flat on my face, with my snowshoes tangled. Hopping up, I glance around, sweat dripping from my armpits. I race toward the trees, knowing I'll never make it in time.

A crack sounds, renting the air. My mouth falls open, and I let out a scream, lifting my legs, slogging through snow. My muscles burn, but I push harder, running for my life. A snowshoe comes undone and dangles, tripping me, and I bend to pull it off, sinking deep into the snow. I'm stuck in the open snowfield.

A whoomph and a roar makes me look up and gasp. A mass of snow high above cleaves from the mountain and comes tumbling in a rushing river of white, kicking up clouds of snow, barreling down.

I jerk my head and search for a safe place, but I'm exposed, with nowhere to hide. Compared to this mighty mountain, I'm nothing at all.

White thunder roars, growing louder. Boulders tumble, booming and cracking, coming toward me. Earth shifts under my feet. A tidal wave of torrential white snow roars closer. I set off the beacon and dive in the snow, covering my mouth.

43

———

JACKLYN

I stand at the front window and watch my neighbor Zoila stride by my house with a raccoon trailing her ten feet back. She sashays and swings her hips, wiggling her fingers at me and smiling with white teeth. Everything about her is perfect, suspiciously so.

Mercury comes up to me and peers out. "Quite the view, isn't it?"

My back straightens as stiff as a board, and I cross my arms. "If you like that sort of thing."

He pats my shoulder and kisses my cheek. "Sweetheart, you're the best thing that happened to me in a long time. You're more than enough for me."

Jerking my head away from the window, I smile at him. "Same to you, my dear."

44

KELLY

I flop on my bed, beat my pillow with my fists and cry ugly tears, sobbing. I've lost my best friend by cutting her out, and she's rightfully hurt. I used her and her house to get what I wanted, a cover for sneaking around.

I reach for my phone and remember Mom took it. Shaking my head, I can't imagine existing without the device. It's like a body part. I'm naked without it.

I blow my nose, honking like a goose, just like my dad. I need to apologize to Plum and her mom. I'm utterly devastated and sorry I hurt them.

I hop out of bed and sit at my desk to write an apology card. But the words don't come, and all that's left is a gut-grinding guilt eating away at my stomach. I peek out the door to see if Mom is hovering nearby and tiptoe to the bathroom to take a shower.

But when I undress, my mouth falls open. My whip is gone. It comes back to me that I gave it away and now it's lost.

I turn on the shower and wail into the torrent of water, washing my dirty hair and stinking body. I misled Mom into believing the falsehood that Granddad's taking me was his idea. And I lied saying I was staying at Plum's. That's a stack of lies already. When will the list end?

I turn off the water and towel dry, patting my arms and legs. The clothes I wore last night sit in a smelly pile on the floor, reeking of my sins, and I never want to see them again. I hurry to my room to dress and have the Big Talk with my mother.

45

JACKLYN

I call Irena to talk about the city planning department's requirement for an environmental survey and my meeting with the banker, but before I get more than a few words out of my mouth, she says this isn't a good time.

I charge ahead, undaunted. "But you wouldn't believe what's going on with the building permit. Not only do I need investors, and the bank wants to charge me a big fat interest rate, but the loan has a five-year call and a balloon payment. Can you believe it?"

Irena sighs.

I say, "I was thinking your friend Tex might be interested in investing in Stone Estates. Would it be okay if I contacted her? Can I have her digits?

Irena says, "I don't want to bother her. She's busy

helping me with my company, and it wouldn't be fair for you to ask her for a handout right after she gave me money."

"But you said she's wealthy and interested in investing in new opportunities. This would be perfect for her."

"I'd love to help you, but this isn't the time. I can't give out her contact information, since she and I just started working together. She's quite controlling anyway, so I'm not sure she's the type of person you want nosing around in your business and telling you know to do things."

I huff. "I'm flexible and open to new ideas. I'm not stuck in my ways, but it would really be Tex's decision if she wanted to invest or not. But you sound tense. Is something wrong?"

"Kelly lied to me and went out all last night, but I don't know where. It's breaking my heart. My little girl turned into a trouble maker, all of a sudden."

"I can come over and talk to her. Do you think that would help?"

She pauses. "I'll keep that in mind, but not now, thanks. I need to get some answers from her first. And I want to call Jack and let him know what's going on."

"Good luck. I'll be thinking of you. I love that girl and will do anything I can to help her."

We hang up, and I scold myself for blathering away when she didn't want to talk. I've got to rein in my obsession with my building project. If I don't, friends won't pick up the phone when I call, and they'll turn around and go the other way if they see me coming down the sidewalk.

Buddy barks and yips in the back yard, and I frown. His high-pitched yelp sounds frightened. My pulse races, and I grab my walking stick, rushing out into the wind and rain.

A raccoon, with its teeth bared and claws swiping, is charging at Buddy, who growls and snaps. His hackles are up like I've never seen before.

I scream and swing the stick down between them. "Get. Out. Of. Here. Go."

The raccoon charges again at my dog, and I wave the stick at it. "Git."

It gives a last growl and runs away, climbing the fence and going up a fir tree. Another raccoon watches from the base of a maple tree. Buddy growls and I drag him in the house by the collar. "Come on, let's go."

Closing the door, my hands tremble, and I check him for injuries. Examining his face, head and haunches, I say, "You came away unscathed this time, but next time you might not be so lucky. I'm going to do something about the raccoon situation before you get hurt."

I call animal control and complain about Buddy's wildlife encounter. "Can't you do something about the raccoons? There are more and more of them in my yard, and one just attacked my dog."

The female officer says in a calm voice, "There's no

rule against feeding raccoons. But you can hire a trapper if you like. Look on the state fish and wildlife website for trappers listed there."

I hang up and find a trapper named Eric who lives in a nearby town. When he answers, I say, "A raccoon just attacked my dog. My neighbor feeds them, and more of them are coming here. It's dangerous." I peer out a window at five raccoons scurrying by.

"I charge a set-up fee and one-hundred-dollars per animal. That's less than others charge, but I'm not in this to get rich. This is my second job."

I glance at Buddy, panting on the floor. "I'm worried about my dog."

"Raccoons can carry canine distemper and rabies, and it isn't healthy to have so many of them in a small area."

I let out a sigh. "I guess I can pay you or the vet if my dog gets hurt, so let's go ahead. How soon can you get here?"

"I'll come over in a few hours to set traps, and you'll pay when we're done."

"Thank you. I'll see you then."

I hang up and cross my arms, staring outside. "Help is on the way, Buddy. They're cute creatures, and I don't like doing this, but it's getting dangerous with so many of them."

I pull on my puffer jacket, put my phone in my pocket and tell Buddy, "Stay here. I'll be right back."

Taking the walking stick, I step out of my house and scan the area. Two raccoons are sitting by a salal bush. One looks down from a tree as I proceed next door.

In my neighbor's yard, five raccoons sit on the grass, watching her house. I tromp up the steps and ring the doorbell. Zoila answers and says in a breathy voice, "Can I help you?"

I nod. "Please, stop feeding the wildlife. My dog was just attacked by a raccoon."

She shrugs. "I'm not going to do that. Anything else?"

"I just wanted to let you know I called a trapper, and he'll be here to assess the raccoon problem. I saw eleven of them on my way here. The trapper said it's not safe to have so many in one place. If there were just a few it would be fine."

She frowns. "They're not hurting anyone. They have a right to exist, just like we do."

"I agree, and I hate to do this. But this many can carry disease, and one attacked my dog. Did you hear about the woman who fed raccoons and there were so many, she couldn't leave her house and had to call 911?"

She wrinkles her nose and shuts the door in my face.

I shake my head at how we see things so differently and march home, closing the door and calling Mercury to report on the latest upheaval in my life.

He says, "You've got troubles coming every which way, don't you?"

"I do."

"Anything I can do to help?"

"Just having you as a friend is enough."

An hour later, a black unmarked truck backs into my driveway, and a man in a tan work jacket, ball cap and jeans climbs out. Buddy barks, but I leave him inside and go greet the trapper.

Shivering in my puffer jacket, I say, "I'm Jacklyn."

"Eric." He extends a hand, and we shake. His grip is firm, and his ruddy face is weathered. "You've got a problem, from what I gather."

I point to Zoila's house. "My neighbor feeds the raccoons, and she won't stop. I've counted eleven of them today, but there may be more."

He glances at Zoila's house. "Did you tell her I was coming?"

"Yes."

He nods. "I'll take a look around and leave traps. I see they're made a trail in your yard. Do you leave pet food or water outside?"

"Not food, but there's a bowl of water."

"Take it inside. I think I can take care of your problem."

I cross my arms, wishing I wasn't in this situation and wondering if I'm overreacting. But then I remember how Buddy was attacked. "Okay, let's go ahead."

He says, "After I'm gone, if you see an animal in a trap,

text me, and I'll come over right away. If I don't reply within a few minutes, call me."

"I will." Walking away, I take Buddy's water bowl inside and watch from a dining room window as he sets out three traps. He climbs in his truck, and I wave goodbye as he drives away. A raccoon climbs the fence, going in the yard, and two more scurry by, confirming my decision. It is so sad that feeding these wild animals is not helping them. People are causing the problem, not the raccoons. Who wouldn't want to live in a place where they get free food and water?

My neighbor Bernard Frackus comes up the front walkway and knocks. When I open it and gesture for him to come inside, he adjusts his black-framed glasses and says, "Thanks, but I don't have time to come in. Have you noticed all the raccoons? They started showing up around the time the new neighbor moved in."

I open my hands. "It's nuts. One of them attacked Buddy, so I called a trapper. He just left."

Bernard nods. "He was in the black pickup?"

"Yes, and it's going to cost me plenty to get rid of them."

He cocks his head. "Tell you what, I'll talk to the neighbors about chipping in. This is more than your problem. It impacts all of us."

We say goodbye, and I close the door, settling on the sofa to read a book. Buddy hops up next to me and turns in a circle, plopping down with the white tip of his tail touching his nose.

I pat his soft head and say, "You sweetie, you. I'm glad you weren't hurt. It scared the daylights out of me."

Buddy sits up, tilting his head, as if listening to something. Hurrying to a window, I see a raccoon in a trap. Buddy paces, and I text the trapper. 'A raccoon is in a trap.'

He replies, 'I'll be over in thirty minutes.'

46

IRENA

I clench my jaw and pace the floor. I want to shake Kelly and shout at her. I don't understand why she lied to me. Whatever her reasons, Jack needs to know what she did and be included in our discussion. As her father, he'll be concerned.

Water runs in the bathroom, and Kelly must be taking a shower. I call Jack and when he answers, I say in a tight voice, "Kelly wasn't where she said she'd be last night. I'm really worried about her."

"Where was she?"

I stare out the kitchen window. "I'm not sure, but I'm about to find out. We're about to have a talk, and I'm dreading what I'll hear. Do you want to listen in when she tells me, assuming she coughs up the truth?"

"I need to help Abby, because she just woke up. Can

you come over here in an hour? I'd like to hear directly from Kelly about this."

'We'll be there. Oh, and Jack?'

"Yeah."

"When we were kids, we were wild, but I have a feeling what she did was worse."

He whistles and says in a low voice, "That's saying a lot. See you later."

I knock on Kelly's bedroom door and go in. She's sitting on her bed with her legs crossed and her eyes closed, meditating like Abby taught her. I perch on the edge of the mattress and count the seconds, slowing my breath.

Her eyes flash open and she moves back, leaning against the wall. "I'm sorry I scared you."

I scoot closer to her and pat the bedspread. "Hon, we love you, your dad and Abby and I. We don't want anything bad to happen to you."

She chokes up, sniffing and wiping her eyes. "Well, it's too late for that. Bad things already happened to me."

I nod. "They did. I know that and I realize it's a difficult time for you."

"Difficult is an understatement, Mom. I feel like a stranger in my body and my mind. I'm not the same."

Reaching over, I open my arms and embrace her. She leans in and her shoulders shudder. She says, "I wanted to try something new, to be daring and do dangerous things. But it was scary." She pulls away, blowing her nose.

I touch the tip of her nose and say, "I love you, sweet girl, and I always will, no matter what you do. I want to know what you were up to and what you did. Tell me everything."

She picks at the quilt, the one hand-stitched by my mother before she passed away. I wait, and finally she releases a breath and begins to tell me her story.

"I was with two girls from school, Avery and Vista. They're in my class but not part of the regular group. I feel screwed up now and thought they'd understand. People like Plum don't get how messed up it was and how terrified I was with Granddad. I thought I'd never see you again."

I squeeze her hand. "And?"

"It wasn't like I thought it would work out. They drank booze, and I did too. It tasted awful, but it made me feel good for a while."

My stomach churns at the thought of my thirteen-year-old drinking with those girls. But I hold my breath and keep quiet, so she'll continue.

"And then we ran out into traffic on Highway 20."

My mouth falls open. "What?"

She nods. "It wasn't as much fun as I expected. We were weaving in and out of cars, laughing and dizzy, and cars honked. People yelled at us."

My throat is dry, and I swallow. "Did anyone offer to take you home or stop to talk to you? Did a police officer come by?"

She shakes her head. "One girl got taken home. The worst thing is, I lost my whip."

My eyebrows shoot up. "Your whip? I didn't know you had one."

She crosses her arms. "I took it from Granddad and used it to keep him away from me at that store, until the State troopers arrived."

I rest a hand on my acidic stomach. What she went through when she was kidnapped is even more traumatic than I realized. I must tread lightly, because if I push too hard, I'll create distance between us. I say, "You liked having a whip?"

"Yeah, I liked having it because it made me feel safe."

"Thanks for telling me this. And then what happened?"

She shrugs. "I was tired and couldn't go to Plum's that late, and I didn't want to come home and have you yell at me, so Avery took me home."

I purse my lips and think fast. I must be careful with my words right now. I don't want what I say to make her shut down and stop sharing about what happened last night. "How was that, staying with Avery?" I want to probe for details about Avery's family, the state of the home, where it was located, but I press my lips together. There will be a time for grilling down deeper later on, if she continues to open up.

She wrinkles her nose. "It was disgusting and gross and I threw up outside on the bushes by their front porch.

Her dad stayed in the bathroom in the morning, and I never saw him."

A chill passes over me, and my hands clench, imagining my daughter of a tender age out on her own with people I don't know. She scoots over and leans into me. "Mom, it was awful. I thought I'd have this big adventure but it was a total nightmare. And worst of all, I lost Plum as a friend. She won't speak to me now."

I run a hand down her wet hair and say in a soft voice, "You never know, she might come back to you. Did you apologize?"

"I did, but she shut the door in my face."

I sigh. Friendship drama among girls is a fraught territory with hidden dangers and daggers. I'm not the best one to guide her through this murky mess, because I was an odd ball, the last girl to be picked for teams or asked to come to sleepovers. But I'll do my best. "Give her time. Maybe make her a card saying you're sorry and leave it at their house."

She pulls away from me and lowers her legs, sitting on the edge of the bed, so I join her. Everything I thought I knew about Kelly seems to be turned upside down.

She says, "Her mom is mad at me too. Maybe I'll wait a while to do that."

I rub her back. "That's a good idea. I'll speak with her mom. But what about seeing those two girls again? Are you tempted to hang out with them and repeat what you did?"

She says in a forceful voice, "No, it wasn't fun. It was dangerous and not in a good way." She's silent for a moment and looks over at me. "Can I see that counsellor we met at Abby's?"

I smile, relieved she's finally willing to talk to a therapist about her ordeal when she was taken by her grandfather. Nudging her with my elbow, I say, "You mean Gladys Knight? That counsellor?"

Kelly breaks into a tentative smile. "Yeah, that one."

"I'll give her a call and set something up."

"Good."

"You know I'm always here for you, right?"

She swallows. "Yeah."

I rub her back. "And you can tell me anything."

"Yeah."

Blowing out a breath, I stand and stretch my arms to release some of the tension I've been holding inside since she wasn't at Plum's house. "Anything else you want to say?"

She gets up and touches her hip, wrinkling her forehead. "I hurt my leg when I fell last night. My hip hurts." She rests a hand on it and frowns.

I wince. "Is it difficult to walk?"

She shifts on her feet. "I'm okay for now."

"I'll take you to see a doctor."

"I'm fine."

I clear my throat. "You father is very concerned, and

he and Abby want to see you and hear what you did last night."

She groans and looks down, studying the floor. "I don't want to. I thought telling you was enough, and that you'd tell them."

Placing my hands lightly on her shoulders, I look her in the eyes. "Your father loves you and wants to hear what happened. He asked us to come over."

She scuffs a bare foot on the floor. "I'm really tired from being up all night. Can't we go at another time? I'm going back to bed."

Resting a hand on the cool metal doorknob, I shake my head. "You can do that later, when we get home. We're leaving right away, so you can eat in the car. We're due at their place in ten minutes."

She flops on her bed and groans, holding her head. "Ten minutes? I'm tired. I want to go back to bed and sleep."

"Let's go. Up and at 'em. You dad's waiting to see you."

She whines. "Please, Mom. I need to sleep. My head hurts."

"See you in five in the kitchen. I'll make the toast."

She moans.

I hurry into the kitchen, pop two slices in the toaster and hope things will go well at Jack and Abby's. The dog whimpers, and I pet his head. "Everything's going to be okay. We're going to see Jack and Abby. You'll like living with them when they get better. In the meantime, you're part of our pack."

Happy smiles and pants, and I have him sit, giving him a treat. A piece of toast pops up, and Kelly comes in the kitchen. Her hair is brushed, and she opens her arms. "Come here, Happy."

The dog trots over, and she hugs him, and I smile, hoping everything will be all right. It'll just take time. She looks up. "Mom, I don't want to go back to school. I don't like it there anymore."

My mouth falls open. "We'll talk about it later. Grab your toast. We need to go."

She groans, picking up the toast. "Whenever you say that, nothing happens. It's your excuse to put something off if you don't like it."

"You dad is waiting, let's go."

We take the dog and hurry out through the rain to the car, piling in and closing the doors. The inside of the car smells of dry toast, damp dog fur and strawberry shampoo. Kelly crunches and chews on the way to Jack and Abby's, while I absorb what she told me about not wanting to go to school.

Tears threaten to fall from my eyes, but I blink them back and park out front my friends' place. The dog barks and whines, and Kelly lets him out. He runs to the front door, clawing to get in and see Jack, one of his favorite people. I follow in Kelly's wake, worrying and wondering how this discussion with her dad will go.

47

JACK

I lean on a cane and make my way to the door, letting Kelly in. The dog bounds inside, nearly knocking me over. I've been weak since I got out of the hospital for a head injury, and it has taken all my energy to care for my new bride in the wake of her car accident in a recent snowstorm.

Kelly goes over and hugs Abby, who is seated in a recliner with the leg rest raised. Abby's broken arm is in a sling, her broken leg is in a cast, and she has a jagged scar on her face. We're a pair of hobbling old forty-year-old fools.

Irena breezes in like she owns the place, which is her approach to life. But as her ex-husband, I know that deep within, she's as insecure as the rest of us and she is sad about the way she grew up, with a mom who worked two jobs and was rarely at home.

I study Irena's face, because instead of her usual grin, her lips are pressed together and her cheeks are wet with tears. She wipes her face before giving me a hug. "Hey, Jack, how are you doing?"

I gesture to the cane and point to Abby. "Hanging in there. Want anything to drink?"

Kelly says, "I'd like lemonade, if you have it. And water or coffee for Mom."

Irena waves a hand in front of her face. "I'm fine for now. I'll pass." She settles in a chair and sits straight up. Something is definitely wrong. I put a hand to my chest and hope I can bear the bad news about what Kelly was doing last night.

Abby meets my eyes. She can see it too. The whole vibe in the room is off, and tension is mounting. Irena picks at a cuticle, and Kelly comes back into the room with a glass of lemonade from a pitcher I made just for her. Her visits here are fairly rare, but we have a vacant bedroom upstairs that's hers whenever she decides to use it.

Kelly turns to Abby. "Can I get you anything?"

Abby's hand trembles. "Thanks, I'm fine."

"Dad?"

"No, thanks," I say. "Let's get started. Why weren't you where you said you'd be? Tell me all about it. Just spill the beans and tell Abby and me everything."

Kelly taps a fingernail on the glass of lemonade, and we wait for her to speak. The room grows quiet, and I squirm in my armchair. A delivery truck rumbles by. A car door slams outside. The dog barks when the mail carrier tromps up the front steps and shoves mail through the slot.

I pet the dog and hold my breath, waiting for Kelly to surrender to the silence and speak. Finally, she opens her mouth. "It's tough to talk about, really. I don't want to."

We grown-ups, who still feel like kids, nod and wait.

She gulps, and words tumble from her mouth, freed from whatever she was thinking. "I guess I've been pretty messed up since Buzz was supposed to marry Mom, but he didn't, and he died. And it turned out he hurt you, Dad, and I was so confused."

I cringe, recalling how my best friend hit me in the head and caused my traumatic brain injury and left me for dead on a dark night on a dead-end road. I was lucky and lived, but he jumped off a bridge and disappeared. I don't think about him that often anymore, except when my head hurts or I can't remember an event or person from my past. A headache throbs, reminding me of what's best left forgotten.

Abby nods. "I get that. What he did confused all of us. What else haven't you told us?"

A lump forms in my throat. I'm grateful my new wife is such a good stepmother. She's perfect in every way, and I tell her that each day when I bring her coffee in bed.

Kelly drinks the rest of her lemonade, and I get the feeling she's stalling before telling us something important. She sucks in a deep breath and blurts out, "I hate my school. I hate my teacher. I hate the other kids, except for Plum. I don't fit in anymore with anyone."

"Oh, hon," Irena says. "That sounds tough."

Kelly nods and tears slide down her cheeks. "It is."

Abby chimes in. "Sounds like you must feel left out and lonely and alone in a sea of people."

Kelly says in a choked voice, "Yeah, that's it."

Abby says in a soothing tone, "I felt that way at your age. Let's talk about it later. But tell us where you were instead of at Plum's place and who you were with."

I sigh and issue a silent thanks to Abby for carrying the load of this heavy conversation. I get the feeling from Abby and Irena that before my bout of amnesia, I wasn't a very responsible guy. I might have been a deadbeat dad, from what they've described, but they haven't used those exact words. I'm going to start making the missing child support payments to Irena, but before I can, I need Abby to get better, so she doesn't need help. And I want to get trained for a job working in a hospital.

Kelly launches into a stream of words, relaying what happened and where and who she was with.

Abby wrinkles her nose. "Avery's dad? You stayed at his house?"

"Yeah. What about him?"

Abby looks at Irena and me. "Remember him in high school? How he sold pot beneath the football field bleachers during school?"

I shrug. "I don't remember. You could tell me I was on Mars back then, and I'd believe it."

Abby half-smiles. "That's right. You don't remember. Irena, how about you?"

Irena looks up from pushing on a cuticle. "I remember him."

Abby says, "He went on to selling cocaine and was arrested, spent time in prison. Was anyone else hanging around the house when you were there?"

My daughter frowns. "Don't know. I didn't look around the place."

I say, "Might be best if you avoided that house from now on."

Irena glances around the room. "All of us are guilty of one crime or another. We're lucky we're not all in jail." My jaw drops and I wish she'd stop, but she continues. "Jack, you were in on a scam."

I hold up a trembling hand. "Hey, wait a minute. I was an informant for the FBI."

She shakes a finger. "But you were party to fraudulent activities."

Kelly says, "Mom, stop. What are you doing?"

Irena turns on Abby, whose face pales. "And we know what you used to do. And I have my own problems, being obsessed with my business. My point is, we're all guilty, and we're lucky to be sitting here, supporting Kelly. Let's not judge others."

I sit back, furrowing my eyebrows. Something is

going on with Irena and I'm not sure why she's acting like this. Maybe I'll find out later when Kelly isn't around.

Kelly says, "Mom, you're acting weird." She says to me, "I know to stay away from Avery's house from now on. I didn't like it there, and I ran all the way to Plum's, but she won't speak to me now."

Abby pats the arm of the recliner. "It sounds like you suffered repercussions from what you did. Irena, what consequences did you give her?"

Irena says in a steady voice, "She's grounded for a month with no devices."

Kelly groans, and I say, "Doesn't she need her phone? What if she needs to call you for a ride or if she's in trouble?"

Irena scowls. "What do you suggest? Have any better ideas?"

I say, "Abby, don't we have an old flip phone you can only use for calls?"

She nods. "Sure, it's in the junk drawer in the kitchen by the microwave. Go find it, Kelly. You can use it."

She rolls her eyes. "Great, now I'll be a loner, a loser, and a weirdo with a flip phone."

I chuckle out of nervousness. "You'll set a new trend and be on the cutting edge."

"Right, Dad." She stomps out of the room, and the dog follows her.

Abby says in a low voice to Irena and me, "Let's talk

later without her here. She's unhappy. We need to do something about it."

"I agree," Irena says. "She's agreed to go to counselling."

I clear my throat. "Let's come up with other ideas too."

Kelly comes in the room. "Are you taking about me behind my back?"

Abby says, "I think you can expect that from now on, given what you did."

"Great," my daughter says. "Now I've got the parent police patrol whispering about me, planning things for me that I don't want to do."

I change the subject to break the tension and tone of the conversation. "Kelly, how are dance lessons going?"

She turns to the window. "I'm not interested in them anymore."

I lean forward. "Why not?"

"It's fake, with forced smiling and dancing around. Life isn't like that. It hurts."

I gasp, and Irena dabs her eyes with a tissue. With Kelly's new defeated, depressed attitude, I can see why Irena looks so down.

Abby says, "Hang in there, kid, we'll turn this ship around. Right, Irena?"

Irena sighs and rallies, rising to the challenge. "Yeah, we'll pull up anchor, hoist the sails and set a course for freedom and happiness, avoiding submerged rocks along the way."

Kelly smiles, looking at us. "You're all crazy." The dog licks her hand, and she leans down and pets him.

I stand and give Kelly a hug, and she leans into me. With my arms around her, I whisper in her ear, "It'll turn out all right. Just give it time. Wait and see."

She steps back. "I know you mean well, but I don't want to wait. I want it to be better right now. It hurts too much."

She buries her head in my chest and sobs, melting my heart. If I could wound, maim and kill Irena's father for what he did to my daughter, I would. But he's in a small town south of us and about to be locked up in prison for the rest of his life.

I grimace and pat my daughter's back. The bastard took the very best part of us and ruined her innocent outlook on life. It will be a long time until she trusts someone again and that includes family.

48

DUSTY

I try swimming with snow rushing past to stay on top of it, but the snowpack pins me down. Clawing at snow, I dig out an air pocket in front of my face, but I can't tell which way is up. The weight of the snow presses down on my chest.

My legs are stuck, and I can't move them.

I gasp for air, but there's not enough oxygen. I'm hungry for air. The mountain I disrespected is killing me, and I can barely breathe. What a fool I was to think I was immortal. I see Dad looking down, frowning.

Sorry, Dad, I didn't do better.

Sorry I failed you and Mom.

Sorry I wasn't a better man.

Snow welcomes me in a silent embrace, wrapping me in a frigid death grip, and I surrender to the shroud of what's beyond, passing out.

49

ZOILA

I call Kirk, and when he doesn't pick up, I send him a text. 'See you at 1. Remember you promised to take me to the cancer care center then.'

I wait for his reply and little dots appear, but no message comes through. He must not have seen my text or heard my phone call. I pull on a warm coat and rush outside, striding to Kirk's and knocking on the door.

Kirk's wife comes to the door, and she isn't smiling. She says, "Can I help you?"

"Yes, Kirk promised to take me to the cancer center today for treatment at one. It's infusion day. He drops me off and comes back for me."

Kirk's wife studies me. "Your hair hasn't fallen out. Why is that?"

I play with a strand of hair, wrapping it around my finger. "This is a wig. It's a high-end one, so it looks real.

And that wasn't very nice of you. I need support during this difficult time, and I was hoping I could count on both of you for support, since we live next door to each other."

She crosses her arms. "Kirk is on a conference call and told me not to interrupt him, no matter what."

"But he promised to take me, like he always does."

She shrugs. "Sorry. I guess you'll have to find another way there. Take an Uber?"

I stomp a foot. "I want Kirk to drive me."

She opens the door slowly. "Come on in. I'll take you."

She puts on her coat, takes her purse, and we head out through the rain to her car. I clench my teeth and sit in the passenger seat. This isn't how I saw it going, not at all.

Her stern voice breaks into my thoughts. "Tell me what you do for work. I must have heard Kirk tell me, but I've forgotten."

I stare out the side window. "Oh, a little of this, and a little of that."

"Well, whatever you're up to, make sure it's not with my husband."

I gulp. She's onto me, and I'll have to be more careful.

50

JENNA, KIRK'S WIFE

Rain hits the windshield as I drive and form a plan. Zoila points to the curb in front of the cancer care center. "You can just drop me off there."

Something about her manner and her underlying nervousness makes me suspicious, so I find a parking spot nearby instead of dropping her off. Zoila hops out of the car. "Thanks, see you later," she says with a white-toothed smile.

"Hold on, I'll go in with you." I hop out of the car and follow her inside.

"You don't have to come in. Kirk never does that."

"I'd like to see the place. I've always wondered what it's like inside. Are the chairs comfortable?"

She hesitates. "Sure, I guess. Yeah, of course."

We step into the lobby and go up to a reception desk.

Zoila stops and turns to me. "Only patients are allowed beyond this point."

I gesture to a waiting area with upholstered chairs. "I'll sit and wait. I'll be here when you're finished to take you home."

She issues a defeated sigh. "Whatever."

She disappears behind a door, and I wish it was the last I'd see of her back, but I won't be so lucky today. My plan will take time to activate and make her move away and out of my husband's eyesight. I've seen him standing close to her inside her house when he was called over to fix a dripping faucet or some nonsense. I smile, because when I'm finished, she won't be batting her eyelashes at him. She'll be long gone.

My phone dings with a text. Kirk writes, 'Where are you? The car is gone. I need to take Zoila to her appointment.'

I grin. 'I took her. I'm here at the cancer center, and I'll bring her home.'

'You did it? I'm surprised.'

I shrug and text back, 'That's what neighbors are for.'

'See you at home. You have a good heart.'

I pocket my phone and a wide smile spreads across my face. If he only knew what's going on inside. I'll protect our marriage from his long-legged siren of an ex-wife. She is manipulating my husband, making him feel sorry for her, and I believe she's faking her disease. I just have to find a way to prove it.

51

IRENA

Kelly and I return home. As we walk in the door, I say, "Want to watch a movie?" She shakes her head and yawns. "I'm going to bed."

She shuffles down the hall, and I remind myself to check her feet from cuts sustained when she was kidnapped. I've got to arrange a doctor visit for her and an appointment to see a therapist. I text the therapist we met at Abby's, who seemed nice and kind and wise, all the things you want in a person who will listen to your darkest secrets.

The phone for Gladys Knight, the counsellor, gives me an automatic message that she's turned notifications off. I massage my temples and make a wish for an easy time when everything doesn't feel like I'm bailing water from a sinking boat with a teaspoon.

Kelly stumbles out of her room and runs into my arms, sobbing. Her shoulders heave, and I hold her tight, rubbing her back. I say, "What's wrong? What happened?"

She pulls away and says in weepy voice, "They're making fun of me online. I can't take it. I'm going to jump off the Jackson Bridge, like Buzz did."

I put my hands on her shoulders and hold her gaze. "Listen to me, you'll do nothing of the sort. We'll get you in to see a counsellor. We'll have you see a doctor. Maybe they can prescribe an antidepressant."

"Mom," she wails in a high-pitched voice. "I'm not a boat to be taken to a shipyard and fixed. This is hopeless."

She leans against the wall and slides down, slumped over and sitting on the floor.

I sit next to her, looking straight ahead, and wonder how our sweet full life came to this moment of angst. "We'll get you through this. You're not alone."

"It feels like it. No one wants to talk to me anymore. They all hate me."

I hand her a tissue, and she blows her nose. I say in a soft voice, "How do you know they're making fun of you? You don't have your phone."

She moans and puts her head in her hands. "I went online on my laptop. And I took my phone back from you when you weren't looking."

I shake my head at how I was outfoxed. "You can be a victim or the victor here. Which one is it going to be? Are you going to weep and wail and moan because other kids are making fun of you? Or are you going to stand up to them and be proud of who you are?"

"I don't know."

"Think of how my mom was when cancer got her down. Did she whine about it? No. Was she tough? Yes. Be like grandma, when you feel weak and sad. Be proud of yourself and all you've been through. You're an amazing person, and I'm proud to have you as my daughter."

She looks over. "Really?"

"Yes, really. Now give me the phone back before you get grounded for the whole year and another one after that."

She giggles and gets up, handing it to me. The phone buzzes with a text, and she flinches. This girl has been through so much trauma, she doesn't need more heaped on.

Holding up the phone and standing, I say, "How about we just turn it off and block out the negative noise?"

"Okay."

I turn off the device and tuck it in my jeans pocket, glad to be rid of one source of amplified bad feelings. My phone rings, and I see it's the counsellor that Abby recommended. I answer and say, "Hello."

"This is Gladys Knight, returning your call."

"Thanks for calling back. I'm Irena Fishbone, and my daughter Kelly would like to see you for an appointment. We met when you were at my friend Abby Love's apartment. When might you have time?"

"Of course, I remember you, because you accused Abby of stealing sneakers. I have an opening tomorrow at one, because someone just cancelled, but won't Kelly be in school then?"

I glance at my daughter, sitting with her arms crossed. She slouches over, as if protecting her heart, and she's been doing that since she got home after being kidnapped.

I say, "I'm not sure Kelly will be going back to classes."

Kelly nods, and her eyes fill with tears.

The counsellor asks me to be there during the first session, gives me the address, and tells me how much she charges. I suppress a gasp at the cost, but tell myself bringing my daughter back to life is worth any price.

I say, "We'll see you tomorrow. Thanks."

52

JACKLYN

A black truck appears, parking at the curb, and Buddy barks, drawing me to the window. The trapper lumbers out, carrying a red blanket in his hands, and goes over to the trap with a raccoon inside, covered it with a blanket. He picks up the trap, sets it gently in the back of his truck and takes out an empty trap, putting it down and placing marsh mellows inside. He waves goodbye, and I wave back, before he drives away.

An hour later, Buddy paces and whines at the window. I throw on my puffer jacket, grab a walking stick and march out into the rain, walking the perimeter. Two raccoons sit in one cage, two more are in another trap, and one is alone, curled up and napping. I say to them, "You're cute, and I'm sorry."

I text the trapper, and he replies a few minutes later,

saying he'll come by to retrieve, replace and rebait. I start a tally with chicken scratches, noting he has caught six.

Buddy quivers and paces, and I put on his rain jacket, leashing him up. "I can't let you out in the yard with those raccoons prowling around. Let's go for a walk, sweet dog."

We march through puddles, getting our feet wet. Turning toward home, we arrive as the trapper pulls up in his truck. He climbs out and touches the rim of his ball cap, ignoring rain drumming down. He says, "You were right to call me. You've got an incredible infestation. This is a safe environment for them, with food and water. It might take a while to make a dent in this population."

I cringe at the cost and go inside, toweling off Buddy, giving him a treat for being a good dog, and taking off my coat. We settle down in the living room, and I'm in my armchair reading emails on my laptop when a breaking news headline comes through about an avalanche on a mountain near the town of Foothills, where my son lives.

My stomach churns, and I chew on the inside of my cheek. The article mentions warming temperatures and that hikers and climbers were warned about avalanche danger. A search party has been called to find two stranded hikers, who planned their route using artificial intelligence and three-day old weather data, according to friends.

I stare at the empty fireplace, recalling Christmas Eve and years past when my family gathered around and sang songs together. My son could be out there. He talked about snowshoeing on that mountain. He told his sister he'd just gotten a pair of snowshoes, and he was going to Mount Shuksan to write poetry and remember their father.

I snap the laptop shut, call Mercury to tell him what's going on and pace in front of the living room window. Buddy opens an eye and looks on. When Mercury picks up, I say, "There's been an avalanche on the mountain by the cabin where Dusty lives."

"Avalanches happen all the time in the wilderness. Why are you concerned?"

I stare outside, where a raccoon looks out from a cage. Clouds are parting, showing blue sky above. I'm at sea level, but the weather can be quite different in the mountains, where my son might be. "Dusty might be out there."

"Isn't that just a remote possibility? Besides, after the way he treated you on Christmas Eve, I thought you were done with him."

I nod. "I said that, I know, but the pull of the family bond is stronger than the will to hate, at this moment anyway. Remember he mentioned starting a mountain expedition company at our dinner on Christmas Eve? He might be out there on his own and hurt. He might need help."

"But there's small chance of that happening. From what you say, he talks big and has a history of not following through. This might be one of his wild ideas, and he'll never set a foot on a mountain, even though it's almost in his backyard. I think he was telling a story to yank your chain and get attention at the dinner table that night."

"He has lied to me before. I'll think about it."

We say goodbye, and I hang up, texting the trapper. 'One more.'

.

53

JACKLYN

Buddy and I go out on a walk, traipsing through the forest. The novelty of seeing the trapper has come and gone, so I feel free to take a stroll and leave the house while he works. Birds chirp, a breeze blows past and branches on evergreen trees sway.

I smile to myself, because Mercury is right. There's no need to worry about Dusty. He's probably lurking in a bar, mooching off some poor soul to buy him drinks and food, and cooking up a scheme to defraud me of more of my hard-earned dollars.

Buddy stops to sniff a fern, and my phone rings, breaking the peaceful moment. I flinch and the phone flies in the air, but I manage to catch it and answer. Buddy looks up at me with wide eyes, startled. "Hello?"

"Is this Jacklyn Stone?"

"Yes, who is calling?"

"Your name was given by Dusty Stone as his contact person when he was arrested. He didn't show up for his court date today. Do you know where he is?"

I stare through the trees at a boat in the marina, wishing for a time when my kids were young and all was well, or I thought it was, and we were one happy family in the days when my husband was alive. I clear my throat and frown, thinking of my son's home invasion at my house, when I was frightened beyond belief. "I don't know where he is, but he lives in a cabin near the town of Foothills."

"Yes, we have his address. If you hear from him, tell he has an outstanding warrant, and he must schedule a new court date."

I stumble ahead, not noticing my beautiful surroundings any longer. This child of mine keeps messing up. Will he ever grow up and find his way?

Buddy sniffs a salal bush along the trail. We leave the forest and come to a gazebo overlooking the marina, and I plunk down on a worn wood bench. Light dances across gray blue water, and I tell myself to buck up.

Buddy hops up and sits next to me, and I put an arm around him, patting his back. My dog looks up at me and smiles. I say, "I know, everything isn't bad, even if it feels like it. We've got a good life, don't we?"

My phone dings, and Eric, the trapper, texts, 'Removed three. Count is nine.'

I wince, thinking of the money I'll owe the trapper and

the sad situation, where innocent animals were drawn to the neighborhood, congregating in great numbers because someone is feeding them. I reply, 'K'

Looking out at a sailboat going by, I say to my pup, "It's time to do something, isn't it?" I stand, and Buddy jumps off the bench, and we march home, striding with purpose.

Along the way, I call Mercury. "I'm going to join the search party. Dusty might be out there and alone and hurt."

He sounds surprised. "You're not trained in search and rescue. I doubt they'll want hangers on distracting them."

I snort. "I'm not a lookie-loo. I'm family."

"Jacklyn, you don't know if he's on the mountain. He might be in a bar. That's more his style."

I nod and unlock the front door of my bungalow, going inside with Buddy. "You're probably right, but I just have this strange feeling. I'm worried about Dusty."

"Fine, let's go check his cabin first to see if he's there. If he's not, we'll ask around, see if anyone has seen him."

"Good, I'll pick you up in ten minutes, and wear something warm, because we may be going up on the mountain."

"I'll do that, but I'm driving, and no arguments about that. You're distracted, and you wouldn't be safe."

With a shrug, I say, "All right. I wonder if I should bring Buddy, since we might be gone a long time."

"Call Irena and see if we can drop him off there. They have a fenced yard, and Buddy likes their dog."

I nod. "Good idea. I'll call her now."

"See you soon."

54

KELLY

I'm sleeping when I hear the sound of a dog scratching outside my bedroom door. I roll over and try to ignore it, but the sound continues, and two dogs bark. I climb out of bed, stretch my arms and open the bedroom door.

Two dogs bound into the room, bumping into each other, leaping on my bed and jumping off, running around the room. I throw out my hands and laugh harder than I have in a long time.

I crawl in bed, pulling up the covers, and Buddy and Happy jump up, licking my face. I push them away, but they persist, and I break out in a fit of giggles. Buddy rolls on his back, and Happy follows suit. I reach out and pet them, sighing and feeling soft fur.

"Dog therapy, right?" Jacklyn says, leaning against the doorframe. "Works for me."

I give her a shy smile. "Me too, I think."

55

DUSTY

My world is hazy white. I hear voices but can't make out words. My eyelids flutter, and I try to breathe through particles of snow, but I'm oxygen starved.

Crunch, crunch, crunch.

Maybe it's the sound of a shovel digging.

I must be dreaming or dead.

56

SEARCH PARTY MEMBER

I grunt and dig, shoveling snow as fast as I can. Wiping my brow, I say, "I saw this greenhorn on the trail and warned him, but they don't listen, do they?"

A woman with a long braid down her back frowns. "No, they don't. Too many newbies expect a stroll in the park and don't respect the danger the wilderness can bring."

Shoveling deeper, I dig harder, increasing my pace. "We're getting closer. I gave this guy a transmitter. He'd be dead otherwise. We'd never find him."

"What are his chances, you think?"

Panting, I stop to take a breath. "Not good. Any sign of him yet?"

"Nope. Keep digging. Not much farther."

"We're almost there."

57

DUSTY

Strong hands pull me from my cold burial pit. My mouth droops. I can't speak or move a muscle. A man says in a commanding voice, "Let's put him on oxygen."

"Got it," a woman says, slipping something over my head and face. Air whooshes in and out, but my lungs ache. I'm distant and detached, as if my body isn't my own.

They set me on a stretcher. A man says, "Wrap him in blankets."

Firm hands move me around. "Done."

Strapping my useless body down, they carry me on a bumpy ride.

Oxygen forces its way into my lungs.

A woman says, "He breathed snow mist when he was buried. Not good.

The man says, "And he lacked oxygen when he was under. Hope he makes it."

She says, "Seven miles to go until we hit the parking lot."

The coldest cold I've ever known is my bones. If I live, I'll never get warm.

58

JACKLYN

We stop at my son's cabin and knock, looking in the window at a cozy cabin with a wood-burning fireplace, but no one comes to the door.

I call Rose from the cabin at the end of the rutted dirt road. "Have you heard from Dusty lately? He's not at his place near the mountains."

She replies, "Sure, he called and said he was headed up Mount Shuksan today."

My stomach churns with acid. "There was an avalanche there. I'm headed to the park to see what I can find out."

"Let me know what you find out. I bet he's just fine. He might have stopped at a bar or to write poetry along the way."

Mercury and I hop in the car, and he drives, pulling

into a parking lot near where the avalanche happened. I leap out of the car, ready to talk to whoever is in charge and try to join the search party. Mercury calls, "Wait for me."

We stride over to a group that is going up. They're wearing brown jackets with badges that say search and rescue. A North Cascades National Park ranger stands by a sign. She steps in front of me and says, "Only mountain rescue volunteers are allowed up there. No one else."

"But my son might be up there."

She squints at me. "What's his name? Are you sure he was up there today? Was he carrying identification?"

I inhale cool, crisp mountain air. "His name is Dusty Stone, and I'm not sure if he was up there. I don't know if he had ID on him. Call it mother's intuition, but he wasn't at his cabin."

She cocks her head, looking doubtful. "If you're not sure he was on the mountain before the avalanche hit, you need to step aside. We don't need distractions. We've got search and rescue volunteers looking for two parties lost up there."

I bite my lip and push on. "My son is tall and broad-shouldered, He was talking about snowshoeing and starting a trekking company. He might be up there."

Her eyes narrow. "Hold on, he was wearing snow-shoes? Not crampons?"

"Yes, I heard he got them at a yard sale. That's what he

told his sister. He mentioned he was going to try them on the mountain today."

She holds up an index finger. "Just a minute." She confers with another ranger and turns to me. "They're bringing a man down the mountain who was caught in the avalanche. He was snowshoeing and set off an emergency transmitter. You can wait here and see if it's your son."

"Okay," I say in a trembling voice.

Mercury puts his arm around me. "We just have to wait and see is he was up there. I sure hope he wasn't, for his sake."

I lean into him. It would be just like my son to ignore avalanche warnings. Call it mother's intuition, but my gut instinct drew me here to the scene of the search.

I clear my throat and ask the park ranger, "What about the other people up there? How did you know they're lost?"

She shrugs. "They called for help. Planned their route using artificial intelligence a few days ago on their smart phones. Didn't wear proper footgear. They're wearing sneakers. They didn't notice warming conditions on the mountain and ignored avalanche warnings posted over there." She points to a posted yellow sign. "We do our best to warn people before they enter the park, but they traipse past the signs, thinking they know best. Then volunteers have to search for them and bring them out."

I nod. "Thank you for the work you do. We appreciate it."

"We do, " Mercury says.

She says, "It can be life and death on the mountain. People need to respect that."

I let out a tight breath and hope for the best. Dusty and I have had our struggles and challenges, but I don't wish for his death by avalanche. The man being carried down the mountain by rescuers might or might not be my son, but I'll play it out and make sure, hoping everyone makes it out alive.

59

IRENA

I'm grocery shopping with Kelly in the produce section when I get a call from an unknown number. Because it might be a boater who needs a tow, I answer while studying a display of green beans and carrots. Chilly air wafts out, and I reach for a bunch of carrots, but jets spray cold water over the vegetables, getting my hands wet.

A man says, "Hello, is this Irena Fishbone?"

My grip tightens on the phone. I hope this call isn't about my dad, who is in the hospital. "Yes, I'm Irena."

"My name is George Foster, and I'm an attorney in Millersville. I'm calling about some legal matters, and I'd like to meet with you."

I give a quick glance at Kelly, who is picking out potatoes. "What is this about?"

"I'll go over it when we meet. When would be convenient for you?"

Suspecting a scam call, I say in a stern voice, "Who are you really and how did you get my number?"

He sighs. "I'm the attorney for the estate of Bud Wiser, and he named you and your daughter in his will."

I gasp. Kelly comes over, plunking a sack of potatoes in the grocery cart. "Mom, what's wrong?"

My pulse quickens, and I say into the phone, "I'm in the grocery store right now, but we can be there in ten minutes. Will that work?"

"Yes, my office is on Commercial, above the Brown Lantern. I'll see you then."

60

JACKLYN

An ambulance rolls into the parking lot, tires crunching on gravel. Two attendants in blue climb out and confer with park rangers in hushed tones.

Out of the forest, a middle-aged woman and a man appear, trudging down a trail carrying a stretcher with a body. Their faces are flushed, and they are breathing hard. I take a step forward, but a park ranger stops me. "Wait right here."

I cross my fingers and hope my son isn't on that canvas cot litter. The load looks heavy as they tromp the rest of the way down the trail with a body that is still. An oxygen mask covers the person's face.

My heart pounds, my hands clench, and my armpits are damp with sweat, despite cold air wafting off the mountain. My phone dings with a text, and I check it. The trapper says, 'I went by and checked. Up to eleven now.'

I reply, 'Thanks.' I pocket my phone and put the matter out of my mind.

Standing by me, Mercury crosses his arms and taps a toe. Emergency medical technicians unload a gurney from the ambulance and wheel it to the trail head. The two search and rescue volunteers trod down the rest of the trail to the parking lot, hauling what looks like a heavy body on a stretcher.

I let out a tight breath. Staring at the lump on the carry cot, I shake my head. I'm imagining things and jumping to conclusions. My son can't be on that stretcher.

The EMTs transfer what looks like a tall person onto the gurney, and I strain forward to see better. My pulse picks up. I had convinced myself I didn't care anymore about my wayward son, but I do. A small voice in my head chirps, saying what Dusty did can never be forgiven or forgotten, but a mother's love for her child is almost impossible to extinguish.

The park ranger says, "You can go see if that's your son now."

I run over, stumbling on gravel, and stand on shaky legs by the stretcher, gazing down at an ashen faced man with a lantern jaw. His face is gray. I touch his cool cheek and say in a choked voice, "This is my son, Dusty Stone."

I start to hug him, but an EMT steps in. "We've got to

go. We're taking him to the hospital in Mt. Vernon. You can meet us there."

They load the gurney into the ambulance, and I gape at the body until they shut the doors and drive off. A search and rescue volunteer says in a strained voice, "I saw him on the trail and told him not to go up there. But he went anyway. Hope he makes it."

My hands tremble. "Dusty doesn't do what people tell him to. He goes his own way, which may be the death of him today."

The man sighs. "I'm glad I gave him an emergency transmitter. Without that, we might have never found him until the snow thawed, if then."

In a choked voice, I say, "Thank you for all you did. We appreciate it."

Mercury says, "Yes, thank you."

I turn to Mercury. "Let's follow them and get to the hospital."

61

MERCURY

Driving with two hands on the steering wheel, I keep a careful eye on the red boxy emergency vehicle ahead of us. The siren is wailing, and lights are flashing. Cars pull over on the road, making way, and I stay close behind, hunched over the wheel, tailing the ambulance.

Jacklyn stares out the windshield and clenches her hands. "I wonder if he'll live or be brain-damaged from oxygen deprivation."

The emergency vehicle pulls ahead, accelerating at a speed that isn't safe for me to match. I grip the wheel, roaring down the road, and say, "If he was smart enough to make an air pocket around his mouth, I hear the chances of survival are much improved."

She issues a choked chuckle. "Oh, my son is smart, there's no doubt about that. Stubborn, smart and socially stunted fit him to a tee. But what if he can't walk or talk or feed himself? What'll we do then?"

"We'll figure it out. We'll get through this. Why don't you call or text your daughter and tell her they're taking Dusty to the hospital?"

"Good idea." She pulls out her phone, staring at it. "I feel like I'm in a hazy bubble, where this can't be happening. Everything isn't real right now."

"That's what trauma does. Just send a text or call, then you can sit back and relax until we arrive at the hospital."

She dials Rose, but the call doesn't go through. "No cell service here. That's frustrating."

"Cell service stinks in some areas out here, with mountains blocking the signal. We'll call her from the hospital or closer to town."

We pass a small town off the highway and breeze on by. The ambulance is a city block away and creeping farther from us. I check my speed and frown. I can't keep up with their pace. It wouldn't be safe on this two-lane road.

We round a bend, where the landscape opens up. Jacklyn tries calling Rose, but it rings and rings. She hangs up. "I don't want to leave a message about something this important. Bad news shouldn't be left on voice mail messages."

"I agree. Try texting her instead?"

"Seems wrong, but sure. It must be done." She types using her thumbs and, with a whoosh, her message is sent. "Well, that's done. Now I'll sit back and enjoy the ride. Not!"

I let out a choked chuckle and hope this dear woman can dig down and find the strength to get through this ordeal. "Dark humor helps in situations like this. Keep it up."

She reaches over and pats my arm. "I'm glad you're here and hanging in there with me."

"I'm glad to be here with you but wish it was under different circumstances."

We come out of the mountains, getting closer to town. The ambulance pulls ahead, and I can barely see it. With a sigh, I say, "I'm going as fast as I can, but we have to get through this traffic."

She gazes out at the sea of cars. "Everyone is going shopping, but we're in a race against death."

I pull away from a red light and turn toward the hospital. "Strange, isn't it? All these people heading out to shop, but we're worried if a family member will survive."

Her jaw is clenched. "I wish I could hop into another person's reality, but this is what we have to deal with."

I nod, and in my darkest heart, I wish for her son to meet his final end. He's a trouble maker and a constant thorn in her side, only thinking of himself.

I say, "Yep, we'll deal with it."

62

KIRK

I step into the master bathroom when my wife's not around, turn on the tap and call Zoila. I say in a hushed voice, "Don't text or call me anymore or ask me to come over. I think my wife is on to us."

Zoila retorts, "That won't work for me. I love you and want you back."

"I can't keep this up. She'll catch me and kick me out."

"Get a backbone. Don't be a spineless man."

"Watch what you're saying. You don't know what I'm dealing with at work, and now my wife is riding me, watching my every move."

She says slowly, "If things have to change, at the very least, you have to keep taking me to medical appointments and paying for my rent and my treatments. The bill is up for one hundred thousand dollars now."

I gasp and run a trembling hand through my hair.

She hisses, "You owe me for how you left me for her. You promised you'd make it right. You know that, don't you? Or I'll expose you."

I wince, because guilt rides hard on my heart for how I ended our marriage. I was married to Zoila, but met Jenna at a coffee shop and we started talking. I fell in love with her. It just happened. Jenna is the warmest person I've ever met with no guile or deceit, which is not like Zoila at all.

I take a deep breath and shrug off the "should" of my being beholden to her for dropping her and re-marrying within a year. People are allowed to finish a chapter of their lives and move on. "Listen, Zoila, you're not in charge here, I am. And I owe nothing to you. All your power over me is broken. I'm in love with her, and I won't leave her."

"But you still love me, don't you?"

My wife knocks on the bathroom door. "Time for drinks with our friends. They're here."

"Got to go," I whisper into the phone.

"Not so fast, mister. Remember, I know what you did."

I shake my head and hang up, turning off the running water and hurrying down the stairs to the love of my life. The woman I'm married to doesn't play games, like Zoila does, and I know exactly where I stand with her.

Going in the kitchen, where our friends are gathered with cocktails in their hands, I greet them with a wide smile.

63

JENNA, KIRK'S WIFE

I give my husband a glass of red wine, and the four of us clink glasses. Taking a sip of the full-bodied, tart merlot, I swallow and let my eyes flicker over Kirk's countenance, assessing his mood. I heard him talking to someone, most likely Zoila, behind the bathroom door in hushed urgent tones, but now he stands relaxed, shoulders down, chatting with our friends.

But something is still off, I notice, when he shoves a shaking hand in his right pocket. He shifts his weight from side to side and talks a little too fast for cocktail hour conversation. I get the feeling something monumental happened in the conversation up there in the bathroom and I'm dying to know what was said. Would it be stalking if I installed a hidden listening device? No, I have to trust that he's going to come around and do the right thing.

My best friend says something, but I don't hear her.

She taps my arm. "Is everything all right? You look distracted."

I force a wide hostess smile and take a deep breath to calm myself, trying to forget about the worries simmering in the back of my mind. "Everything's great. Let's go sit down and try the appetizers. Artichoke dip, anyone?"

64

JACKLYN

We pull up to the hospital and hurry through sliding doors into the emergency room. Spotting a reception desk, I stand in line to be helped. My thoughts run to when my baby boy was born. I rocked him in my arms and sang to him, but now he's a grown man.

When it is my turn, I say, "I'm here for Dusty Stone, a patient who was admitted by ambulance about fifteen minutes ago. Can we go back and see him?"

She taps on a keyboard and frowns. "I don't show him as admitted yet. You'll have to wait over there with the rest of them."

Mercury and I plunk down into hard plastic seats intended to create discomfort and make a person give up and march away before their turn comes. But we sit and cross our legs, squirm in our seats, stand, and stretch our legs. After almost an hour, I say, "This is ridiculous. I'm going to check with the receptionist again and see if we can join him."

Going up to the reception desk, where a different person is in charge, I say to a man with a pierced nose, "I've been waiting to be with my son, Dusty Stone, and he was brought in by ambulance over an hour ago. Do you have him in your system?"

He types and raises his brows. "He's in the intensive care unit. They're getting him settled in. Wait fifteen minutes and come back for his room number."

I clench my hands. "Could I have the room number now, please, if you know it? We'll go get coffee and take our time moseying up to the ICU."

He glances at me and shrugs. "Sure, he's in Room 712."

I swallow hard and thank him. Irena's ex-husband Jack was in this hospital and treated for head trauma. Crossing my fingers, I hope Dusty won't be brain damaged from oxygen deprivation. Even if he survives being buried by an avalanche, the road before him is unknown.

65

JACKLYN

e find the cafeteria and pay for coffee, punching a button. A machine spits out a black liquid. My hands are cold, and I'm shaking. The room is almost empty, and in a corner, a young woman in blue scrubs with headphones on is eating from a plastic container. Cool air blows from an overhead vent.

I sip the bitter, acidic brew, and my stomach knots. Minutes tick by, and I drum my cold fingers on the table. After what feels like forever but was actually five minutes, I look into Mercury's warm brown eyes and say, "Time to go, don't you think?"

He straightens the blue polka dot bow tie clipped to his long gray beard. "Yep."

We rise and make our way to the elevator, pushing the button for the seventh floor. Time is warped. A fuzzy cloud surrounds my head. All thoughts are silenced. I must see my son.

As we step off the elevator, my pulse quickens. We follow signs to the room, and my phone rings. Rose is calling, and I answer, but a nurse comes by, saying, "No cell phones can be used on this floor. Please put it away. Thank you."

I hold up an index finger to Mercury and go back around the corner, leaning against a corner and speaking to Rose in hushed tones. "I can't talk now, but your brother is in Room 712. We're just about to see him."

"I wish I could be there, but something came up at work. I can't leave now. I'll come up as soon as I can with Max."

I frown. "We're not sure what condition Dusty is in, so it might not be best to have Max visit. I'll let you know what's going on when I know more. Bye. Love you."

"Love you."

Letting out a long sigh, I stride toward Mercury, and we head to Room 712 to hear what the future holds for my son.

66

IRENA

Cold air rushes out when I open the freezer door at the grocery store and put the ice cream container back. We hurry through the self-check-out, roll the cart to the car and unload it in record time. Climbing in the car, I turn to my daughter. "I have no idea what this is about, but here we go." I drive out of the parking lot and look both ways, with the blinker on, even though no one else is coming.

She tilts her head. "Where are we going?"

"Buzz hired an estate attorney, and he named us in his will. We're meeting with him."

"What's an estate attorney?"

I shrug and give her the best answer I can come up with on the spot. "They draw up legal documents for when people die."

Kelly wrinkles her nose. "Who would want to do that? It sounds sad."

A flutter of grief flickers past for my friend who passed away. Buzz had my back since we were kids, when I'd just moved into town. Even though things turned weird at the end, I miss him. Along with Jack, Abby and Craig, we were a pack of long-time close friends. Now, with Craig in prison and Buzz gone, there are only three of us left.

I blow out a breath. "It sounds boring compared to rescuing boats, but it's important work. Someone's got to do it."

I pull up and park near the Brown Lantern, and we get out. Kelly shuts the car door and gives me a smile. "Everything for you is boring except boating."

I grin and nudge her with my elbow. "You're right, except for being your mom. That's the most important part of my life. You know I love you, right?"

She rolls her eyes, and we climb stairs to the second floor, walking down a hallway smelling faintly of cooking odors from the restaurant below. My mouth waters, and my stomach growls. "Let's grab dinner after this. I'm hungry."

She rests a hand on her stomach. "Yeah, me too."

I open the door to the office of George W. Foster, Attorney at Law, and we enter. A receptionist looks up. "Can I help you?"

"I'm Irena Fishbone with my daughter, and we're here to see George Foster."

The receptionist purses her lips and picks up the phone, making a call. Kelly and I walk around the room. I don't want to sit down. I have too much energy.

Maroon upholstered office chairs wait for people with legal problems. Thankfully, that isn't us today. I cross my arms and frown, tapping a toe. I have no idea what we'll hear from the lawyer.

A man in his thirties with a receding hairline comes out and offers his hand. We shake, and he has a firm grip. "Right this way," he says, gesturing down a hall. He leads us into a conference room with a long table and eight chairs. The space has no windows, much like a coffin, but I suppose with legal matters you don't care for a view or fresh air, you just want to get down to business and get it over with.

I swallow hard and take a seat. Kelly sits by me, leaning over. "How long will this take?"

I whisper. "No idea. Sit tight."

The man sits across from us and sets down a stack of papers. He pulls out horn-rimmed glasses and taps an index finger on the table, saying, "I called you here because you have been named beneficiaries for the estate of Bud Wiser. Could I see your identification?"

My eyebrows shoot up, and I open my purse, taking out my driver's license and pushing it across the table to him. He picks it up and examines it. Turning to Kelly, he says, "Do you have any identification on you?"

She shrugs and puts a hand in her pocket, handing

her student identification over to him. He stands, taking them in his hand. "I'll be right back. I'll make copies of these."

He leaves the room, and I glance at Kelly. She's moving her finger over the table top, making imaginary designs. Seconds tick by, turning into minutes. She says in a low voice, "Why is it taking so long?"

I pat her back. "I don't know. Let's wait and see what he has to say."

He strides into the room, hands us our identification and closes the door, taking a seat opposite us. Leaning forward, he says, "Thank you for waiting. You're probably wondering why I called you here. I'll get right to the point."

67

JACKLYN

I peer into the room where my son is supposed to be, but the person in bed is wrapped in layers of insulated blankets. A machine beeps. My phone dings with a text, and I ignore it, because nothing matters more than my son at this moment.

My pulse pounds in my ears, and Mercury holds my hand as we approach the bed. My jaw drops. If this man is my son, he looks half-dead. His face is gray and worn, as if the mountain carved lines into his face. Dusty is thirty-one, but the haggard man before me appears to be fifty-years-old. His chest rises as oxygen fed through a tube forces air into his lungs.

My throat grows tight. This doesn't look like Dusty, but it is. He looks like an older 5.0 version of the son I knew.

I perch on the edge of a chair, wringing my hands, and

Mercury goes to the window, gazing out. A nurse in blue scrubs comes in the room. "Are you family?"

I stand and say in a clear voice, "Yes, I'm his mother."

She eyes me. "He's in critical condition. He has fractured limbs and chest trauma. We are treating him for hypothermia by warming his body and monitoring him for cardiac instability. Oxygen deprivation can cause long-term damage. Tests will tell us more."

I slump into a chair, lacking the strength to stand, and study the stranger in the hospital bed. Coughing away tears, I say, "What are his chances of having a normal life?"

She fiddles with her orange-framed glasses. "It's too soon to know at this point. We're doing all we can for him."

She turns to go, and I say in a choked voice, "Thank you."

68

JACKLYN

Hours later, Mercury and I sit dazed in the hospital room, perched on chairs along the wall, watching and waiting. A wall clock ticks, marking the passing seconds. We are powerless to turn the tide, as my friend Irena might say.

A woman in a white lab coat breezes into the room. Her name tag shows Dr. Abbott, and her long red hair is pulled back in a bun. She glances at Dusty, studies the beeping monitors and turns to me. "You are his mother?"

I stand on weary legs. "Yes, I am. What's wrong with him?"

"We're still doing tests, and we'll know more later today and tomorrow. As soon as he's stable, we'll take him into the operating room, but the risk is too high right now. We need to wait."

I sigh. "I'm not the best at waiting."

She shrugs, and my gaze fixes on a spray of freckles on her face. She says, "Hospitals teach us how to wait for answers. I'll be back."

She leaves, and I slump in a seat by Mercury, asking him, "How are you doing?"

He pockets his phone. "Just fine, considering the circumstances. He's lucky to be alive. I hope he gets better for both of your sakes."

A tear trickles down my cheek. "Me too. We don't need more loss in the family. Not now, and not ever."

My phone rings, and Rose is calling. She says, "I'm on my way with Max but traffic on I-5 is packed. How is Dusty?"

"He's alive, just barely, that's all we know for sure."

"Let me speak to him."

I flinch. "I'm not sure that's a good idea. He's not responsive. He can't speak or open his eyes."

"Please, Mom, just hold up the phone to his ear. I have something I want to say to him."

I shrug and stand. "Okay."

Putting the phone by my son's ear, which has abrasions, I say, "Go ahead, Rose."

She says in a loud voice, "Dusty, wake up and get better. If you don't, I will come and beat some sense into you. Wake up, bro."

I take the phone away, and Rose says, "Bye, Mom." She hangs up.

A flicker of movement under my son's eyelids catches

my attention. I turn to Mercury, who looks up from his phone. "Did you see that? I think he moved his eyes."

A nurse comes in to check his vitals, and I tell her what happened. "Do you think that means he'll be fine?"

Her gaze flicks to Mercury and back to me. "It's too soon to tell."

She leaves the room, and Mercury says, "This is a tough time. Come here. Let me give you a hug."

I glance at the tall man in the hospital bed who is barely recognizable as my son and know that although he has been devious and hurt me, I don't want him to die. I step into Mercury's open arms and let out a long sigh, wrapping my arms around him.

Moments later, my phone dings with a text, and I step back to check my messages, thinking it might be from Rose.

The trapper texts, 'I've trapped fourteen raccoons on your property. My previous record was thirteen. You have an unbelievable infestation.'

My jaw drops, and I nudge Mercury. "The trapper says I have an unbelievable infestation, and he caught fourteen raccoons so far. It's crazy."

He tugs on his gray mustache. "Good thing you called the trapper. That's out of control and not healthy for anyone."

I sigh. "They sure are cute, and it's not their fault. I wish Zoila had never moved in next door."

69

IRENA

I lean in and listen to the estate attorney, curious about why we're here. He says, "As you know, I'm the estate attorney for Bud Wiser, and he named the two of you in his will."

I press my lips together. Maybe if I hold my breath, this will start to feel real. I count to five and exhale, but nothing is different. Buzz, my former boyfriend, is gone, and I'm in a sterile conference room with no art on the walls.

The attorney clears his throat and studies me. "To you, Irena, he left his house, his bookstore and his boat. He said you were the love of his life."

My jaw drops. "His house, his boat and the bookstore?"

He nods, turning his attention to my daughter. "Kelly, he left you his collection of first edition Dickens books bound in leather. He wanted to pass them on to someone who would appreciate them and not sell them."

I turn and check for my daughter's reaction. Old books bound in leather are the probably last thing she wants. She smiles, wiping a tear from her cheek. "I'll take care of the books, but I wish he was still alive."

I whoosh out a breath. "I second that."

After a beat of silence, we take care of paperwork, sign documents, and the attorney hands me the keys to Buzz's boat, bookstore and house.

When he walks us to the door, I cock my head. "Who did he leave all his investments to?"

He looks down at the floor before answering. "He left them to a charity, one that helps children who are bullied by others."

Tears spill from my eyes, and I moan, bending over with my hands on my knees. "He meant well and defended me, and he had a good heart, most of the time."

Kelly says, "But not at the end, when he hurt Dad."

The attorney says, "Well, if that's all, I'll return to my office."

We thank the attorney and hurry down the hall. I blow my nose, and Kelly pats my back, saying, "Mom, are you all right?"

I shake my head. "Do you know what brought Buzz and I together as friends in grade school?"

She shrugs, and we tromp down the stairs. I say, "We were both bullied as kids for our names, and for me, because I was new to town and stuck out as being different."

We come to the bottom of the stairs by the entrance to the restaurant, and a tendril of a delicious cooking odor drifts past. My stomach growls. Kelly sniffs the air and looks at me. "Fries and a burger?"

I give her a hug. "You bet."

We slide into seats on the family-friendly side of the bar and order two bacon burgers with fries. I order a draft beer to celebrate our good fortune, even though it came at the cost of a death of a dear friend. Kelly asks for water, and when the drinks arrive, we raise our glasses and toast. I say, "To our new life. May it be easy and filled with love and laughter."

Kelly grins. "And fun. I don't want a boring life doing drab normal things."

My eyes grow wide. "Then I'd say you're cut out to work in a boat rescue business, with all the drama on the high seas."

She groans and rolls her eyes. "Not that again. You have to stop bringing that up. It only pushes me away from the idea. I'm going to move to Seattle after I finish high school, or maybe before that."

I clench my jaw. "I'd miss you too much. You can't leave my house until you're eighteen."

She sits back and crosses her arms. "You're not the boss of me."

A little voice in my head reminds me that I've just

about ruined our dinner, and I need to dial it back. Back-tracking as fast as I can, I say in a calm voice, "Where would you live if it wasn't with me until you're older? Have you thought about it much?"

She turns her water glass around, staring at it. "I've thought about it a lot since Granddad took me. I don't want to live in town, where kids make fun of me, so even though Dad wants me to move to his house or stay there part of the time, I don't like the idea."

"Duly noted. I get it, and I'm sorry kids are being mean to you. I'll talk to your teacher and the principal."

Her mouth falls open. "No, don't do that. It's be even worse."

Her lower lip trembles, and I say, "Where would you want to live, if not here?"

"On Grand Island, with Tex. Everything is peaceful and beautiful there. She said they have a one-room schoolhouse on the island. I bet I could go there."

I swallow bitter tears and think carefully about what to say next. "I hear you. It is gorgeous there, and she's really nice."

Kelly beams, as if someone turned on a bright light inside her.

I tap the table. "But it's a big deal, and we'd have to ask her. We can't assume she'd be open to the idea. It's a huge responsibility, and I doubt your dad would agree to it. I'll think about it."

Kelly whines. "I'll think about it is what you always say when the answer is no."

A waitperson sets our burgers down with a thud. She says, "Anything else?"

I smile, but inside, my heart is breaking. "No, I think we have everything we need." When the waitperson leaves, I say to Kelly, "I mean it. I'll actually consider it."

Kelly nods. "Good, because I'm miserable. Kids taunt me and call me names. I don't want to live here."

"Aw, hon, I'm so sorry to hear this. I know how that feels."

"Mom, you don't know how it feels. This is different. You weren't kidnapped."

I cut my burger in half and nod. "You're right. It's not the same at all. I'm sorry."

She chomps down on a fry. "What are you going to do with the bookstore?"

"I don't know. I have to think about."

She points at me, grinning. "You said it again. You've got to stop saying that."

I smile. "I love you, Kels. You know that, don't you?"

She takes a big bite of the burger and says with her mouth full, "I know."

Later, I pay and we walk outside. Two girls from school stop on the sidewalk and stand staring, pointing at my daughter and talking in low voices with their hands over their mouths.

I cock my head, clench my fists and say to Kelly, "I'll go

talk to them and straighten them out. Want me to do that?"

She blanches and takes my elbow, pulling me to the car. She jumps in, locks the door and shivers, crossing her arms. "That would only make things worse. Don't do that."

I start the car and frown. "Are you sure?"

"Just drive," she says in an angry voice, looking over her shoulder at the twin-pack of teenage girls. "Let's get out of here and go home."

Heading toward home with a now deflated sense about our news about inheriting from Buzz, I shake my head. I was trapped with taunting kids in a school in a small town, but Kelly is right. What she is going through is far worse. I'll have to find a way to make it better for her before her heart breaks.

70

ROSE

I frown and drive north on the freeway, hands gripping the steering wheel tight. Red taillights glow ahead of us like rubies, and I blow out a breath. Max looks over from the front passenger seat and says, "What's wrong with Uncle Dusty? What happened?"

I swallow hard. "From what I know he went snowshoeing, despite avalanche warnings due to warming weather. He got caught in an avalanche."

"What's an avalanche?"

I tap the brakes when the car ahead slows down and glance at our speed. We're only going five miles an hour and at this rate, it'll take all afternoon to get there. Suppressing a groan, I say to my son, "It's when huge chunks of snow break away from a mountain and come tumbling down."

His big brown eyes look up at me. "Couldn't he have run away?"

I shrug. "I guess not. I don't have all the details, and he's not talking, so we might never know."

"How did he get to the hospital?"

"Emergency medical technicians took him to the hospital."

"Did they dig him out?"

I arch my eyebrows at how curious this kid is. But then again, matters of life and death fascinate humans, maybe because we don't talk much about death, and we expect to go on living forever. When a life is snuffed out in a hiking accident, we're surprised, as if our mortality isn't written into the script of our lives.

"Mom, are you listening? How did they get him out of the snow?"

Inhaling and taking a deep breath of courage, I say, "I don't know for sure, but I think there are brave search and rescue volunteer teams who go into the mountains and find people and dig them out."

"So he almost died?"

I blink back tears. "Yes, and there's a chance he might not make it. He's on life support. You'll see tubes going into his body and machines helping him breathe, so don't be surprised. He might not look much like your Uncle Dusty when we get there."

My son grows silent, looking out the side window, and I bite my lower lip. Shame on my brother for being out there against mountaineering advice. Even I noticed the weather warming news about snow pack conditions and avalanche danger from my place in the city.

I huff out a breath and drive. He shouldn't have been out there. What an idiot. He's caused way too many dust-ups and disasters since our father died. If he lives, it's time for him to grow up and be the man Dad brought him up to be and start using common sense.

Max says, "Do the search and rescue people find dead bodies?"

I slowly exhale. This is turning into a long drive, and I must call on my inner resources to remain a patient, caring, loving parent. "I bet they do, unfortunately."

"How close was Dusty to death?"

"I don't know. Maybe we'll find out when we get there, but pretty close if he's in the intensive care unit and on oxygen. But that's not an appropriate question to ask at the hospital. Remember that. We'll listen, be with Grandma and let her know we love her."

"But I want to ask questions."

"Ask me then and let the nurses and doctors do their work."

"I might want to be a search and rescue person. It sounds important."

I gulp, imagining the dangers they face. "It is important work. You need to get big and strong first, and have some experience in the mountains. You don't want to go out like Uncle Dusty did and ignore dangerous conditions and avalanche warnings."

He sighs. "I won't."

Finally, the freeway opens up when we pass Maryville, and I drive the speed limit. If only Dusty wasn't so self-centered and oblivious to others, we might have had a peaceful household when I was growing up, but our family always accommodated his mood swings, tiptoeing around him when he was grumpy, or chuckling at his bad jokes when he was upbeat. I was so happy to leave that house and move to Seattle to set my own course and not be under the doom dome Dusty held in place over our childhood home.

A short while later, I turn off the highway, heading to the hospital to whatever fate my brother brought upon himself. If he recovers, I'm sure he'll deny bearing any responsibility, which is the way my brother looks at the world. Mom and Dad and I tried, but we discovered there is no changing him. Dusty will be Dusty, no matter what.

71

JACKLYN

The redheaded doctor comes in and looks me in the eye as she says, "Even if your son opens his eyes and becomes conscious, it's possible he may have trouble feeding himself and walking. He may have to rely on a wheelchair to get around."

"Oh, no, Dusty would hate that. He's independent and an active person."

"We'll discharge him when his condition is stable to a rehabilitation skilled nursing facility. Do you have one you'd prefer? Close to your home, so you can visit him?"

An idea crosses my mind, and I say, "Yes, I do. I'd like him to go to Shore Lodge on Cedar Island."

She nods. "I'll make a call to Shore Lodge and see if they have an open bed."

The doctor's orange sneakers squeak on the floor as she walks out of the room.

Mercury says, "That was a surprise to hear. You're sending him to Shore Lodge?"

I shrug. "Sure, why not?"

He raises his eyebrows. "Is this to get back at him for what he did to you?"

My eyes flicker over my son, and I study the floor. I meet Mercury's gaze and say, "If I'm honest with myself, I want to give him a taste of what he dished out to me. Let him see what it's like to be on the other side of a locked door, powerless to go out on your own and breathe fresh air."

He glances at Dusty and nods. "All right, I understand. We'll see how it goes."

Rose breezes into the room with Max. She gives me a hug and touches her brother's hand. Coming over to me, she says in a hushed voice, "How is he?"

His prospects aren't so good," I whisper. "But we're hoping for the best. As soon as he's stable, they'll transfer him to a rehabilitation center."

Rose's face falls. "So, it's really bad, isn't it?"

"I think so."

Max comes over and holds my hand, looking up at me. "What's bad, Grandma?"

I look out the window, blinking back tears. "The traffic is bad, the weather, you name it."

Max says, "When will Uncle Dusty wake up?"

I sigh. "We're not sure. They're doing everything they can."

Rose wipes tears from her cheeks. "I heard of something to do, and I'm going to try it." She marches over to the side of the hospital bed and rests a hand on her brother's shoulder, shaking him. In a loud voice, she says, "Wake up, Dusty. Wake up. It's time for you to open your eyes and wake up."

Silence fills the room. Max shuffles over to his uncle and says in a high-pitched voice, "Wake up, Uncle Dusty. Wake up."

But Dusty doesn't move or blink an eye.

72

IRENA

Driving away from the restaurant and leaving gossiping girls from Kelly's school behind, a thought loops through my mind, and I pull over in front of the used bookstore Buzz left to me. It might be interesting to own a bookstore, but it would require time and attention I don't have. I turn to Kelly, "Come inside with me. For old times' sake."

She shrugs, and we climb out of the car. Lights are on inside, creating a warm glow. Kelly and I walk in, and the smell of dust and old books makes me sneeze. Kelly nudges me. "What are we doing here?"

"Watch and see," I say, going up to the manager, who is writing something down at the cash register. She looks up and smiles. Her red lipstick is bold and bright, outlining a wide, generous mouth. I know her from when Kelly and I came in here in years past.

I say, "Hi, do you have a few minutes to talk in Buzz's office? There's something I'd like to discuss with you."

She nods and a dark look crosses her face when I say the name of her boss and my former boyfriend. It must be a heavy burden to shoulder to run the business after Buzz passed away. She nods to Kelly, who says hello.

She asks an older woman with gray hair to take over the check-out counter before leading us back to what was Buzz's office. The door creaks as she opens it. The office is just like Buzz left it when I saw it last, with smudged windows and a computer and stacks of papers.

We stand in the small space in an awkward gathering. I break the silence by saying, "I don't know if you heard this yet, but Buzz left me the bookstore."

She gasps, claps a hand over her red lips, and tears trickle down her cheeks. "I was afraid this would happen."

I say in a gentle voice, "What did you hope would happen instead?"

"That he'd leave it to me, or the employees, so we could keep it going the same way he ran it. We miss him so much."

I swallow tears, reminded of my long-time friend who is gone. "I miss him too. We all do. I've been thinking it over, and if it's okay with my daughter," looking over at Kelly, who looks confused, "I think it would great if I turned it over to you and the other employees as a profit-sharing entity, where I'd take a small cut, but you'd be in charge of everything."

Kelly nods. "That's okay with me. It makes sense. As long as I can work here someday, if I want to. Would that be all right? I like books."

The manager wipes her eyes and sighs. "When you're old enough to work here, let us know, and we'll train you." She turns to me, giving me a hug. "Thank you. This is such exciting news. I can't wait to tell the others. When will it be official?"

Giving her a tentative smile, I say, "I'll ask the lawyer to draw up papers. I'll let you know more in the next week or so. In the meantime, thank you for keeping the store going. It's a wonderful place."

She sniffs and pulls out a tissue, blowing her nose. "That's it, then?"

I open the door. "For now. See you later. Take care and keep up the good work."

Kelly and I stride outside and jump in the car. She looks over with a smile. "I like what you did back there. Buzz would've liked it."

I grin. My girl is back, for a bit at least. I'll appreciate the flashes of joy flowing from her while bracing for incoming teenage storms that are hovering on the horizon.

73

ZOILA

A black pickup truck parks outside Jacklyn's house, and a man gets out. He glances at my house, tips his ball cap, and I wave, stepping outside and sashaying over to him. Cool air blows past, and I shiver, pulling my cape closed.

I approach the trapper who is taking one of my sweet raccoons away in a cage. A red blanket is thrown over the trap, and he's carrying it to his truck. He sets it down in the back, and I say, "Hello, there. Are you trapping them?"

He nods. "Yes, I am. I'm licensed by the State. You can see my license number right there on the top of the trap."

I pucker my lips, tilting my head, in a move that makes most men succumb to my whims. "It's a shame, what you're doing. Could you let that raccoon go? And the others too? They're beautiful creatures."

"They are, but I've been hired to clear out an infestation. You'll have to take it up with the homeowner, if you have issues. She hired me, and these nuisance animals are on her property."

I wipe rain drops from my face, put my hands together, as if begging, and say in my most innocent, pleading voice, "Please, have a heart. Let these raccoons go back to the wild where they came from. They deserve a happy life."

He shrugs, immune to my charms. "Take it up with the homeowner or the State Fish and Wildlife Department. It's not my battle to fight. I'm just doing my job."

He strides away but glances back as I reach into the truck to undo the trap. But unlatching the cold wet metal trap is much more difficult than I thought it would be, and I can't get it open. The raccoon inside hisses and claws at me, nearly catching my sleeve.

My pulse races, and I pull my hands away, jumping back. The trapper comes over, puts his hands on his hips and glares at me with icy blue eyes. "I wouldn't do that if I were you. You might get hurt, and that trap is my property, and so is my truck. Don't interfere with my equipment. Like I said, take it up with the homeowner or the State. I'm licensed to remove nuisance animals."

A raccoon inside the trap hisses at me and stares. A shiver runs up my spine at how a cute animal has turned into a fierce wild creature, ready to sink its teeth and claws into me. I say with a shrug, "But I was just trying to set it free. It's the right thing to do."

He grunts and slams the back of the truck shut. "We're all entitled to our own opinions. Take it up with the State if you have complaints."

I blow out a breath and stumble back into my house, taking off my damp wig and hanging my wet cape on a hook, where water drops drip on the wood floor. I sink into the couch that Kirk bought me at an expensive home furnishing store, and he told me in secret to never mention the purchase to his wife. I got furniture and paid rent out of the deal, but beyond that, things aren't going the way I planned. I thought his wife would be long gone by now, leaving him to me.

A smile spreads across my face, and I stride into the upstairs bathroom, looking in the mirror. "I've got plans, and no one is going to stop me."

I shave my head and pull on a second wig with long brown hair that I bought at a thrift store. Adjusting it, I screw up my face, because the wig is warm and makes my scalp itch, but the end goal is worth it. I'll fleece my ex-husband, and he won't realize it until too late. As my friend Dusty says, revenge is sweet. Better to be underesti-mated and stick it to them when they least expect it.

74

JENNA, KIRK'S WIFE

I chew on my lower lip and stare out a second-floor window into the house next door, where Zoila is shaving her head. I knew I was right, and she doesn't need to wear a wig. She's tricking my husband and convincing him she's sick, perhaps to get sympathy and attention.

I frown as the thought flits past that Zoila may be cozying up to Kirk with the goal of getting back together with him as a couple, and her becoming his third wife. It has been clear from the start that she resents me and wants him back. She dominates the conversation and flirts with him outrageously, right in front of me, but he doesn't seem to see it that way. I'm not going to be the odd woman out.

The landline rings, and Kirk and I answer it at the same time in different rooms. I can see Zoila in her house on the phone, so I listen and wait for what I'll hear.

"Kirk, honey," Zoila says. "I've been so lonely lately. And I'm sick, so sick, you wouldn't believe it. Chemo is taking a toll and making me throw up."

My husband says in a quiet voice, as if he expects me to walk in at any minute, "I'm not sure what I can do to help you."

"The medical bills are really steep. I can't believe it. I can't begin to pay them."

He says, "I told you already, I'll help you with that."

My jaw drops.

She says, "But it costs so much, and I know you can't afford it. I don't want to burden you with all my troubles."

"Your troubles are my troubles, especially now that you live next door. Whatever it takes, I'll help you out."

My fingers are slick, holding the phone. The nerve of her taking our money, and I bet she isn't even getting treatments.

Zoila says, "Your wife doesn't think I'm sick. But you know I am, don't you?"

"Of course, I do. I believe you, hon. I'm sorry she isn't as sensitive as you'd like."

I grit my teeth and stare at the ceiling.

She whispers, "Do you want to come over and feel my head? My hair is all gone."

"No, I don't want to do that. I love my wife. I can't be carrying on with you."

"But, Kirk?"

"Yeah?"

"My birthday is coming up next weekend, and I'll be lonely and sad if I can't spend it with you."

"You'll be fine. Call an old friend."

"No I won't, and you are my old friend."

"Tell you what, come over that day, and we'll put on a special dinner for you."

My eyebrows shoot up, and I chomp down on the side of my cheek, letting out a little squeak.

She says, "What was that? Is someone else on the line? Is your wife listening to this conversation? She'd better not be."

Kirk tromps up the stairs, and I quickly hang up, hurrying into the bathroom, stripping off my clothes and hopping in the shower. My heart races, and I stand under a flow of tepid water until the hot water comes on.

Clenching my hands, I issue a silent scream. I can't bear being around his ex-wife. When we married, I knew she came along with the package of his past, but now I'm fed up and want to bury her in the backyard.

I can't let her take our money and get away with this scam. He needs to stand up to her and tell her to back off, but if he won't, I will. Three of us in this relationship is one too many. I'm going to expose her and find a way to end this madness.

75

DUSTY

I hear people talking, and I want to talk and open my eyes, move my hands, but my body doesn't respond. The words Shore Lodge are uttered, and I cringe inside. No, not that place. Anything but that. The voices stop, and I disappear, fading into a darker place than I've ever known, not awake and not dreaming.

A tube is pulled from my throat, and I gasp for air. breathing on my own. A machine in the room turns off. A while later, which might be hours or days, hands pick me up and move my body onto what might be a stretcher. They roll me down a hall, but I can't comment, make a wisecrack or fight against it.

They load me into a vehicle, and we bump down roads. Sometime later, we stop. The smell of sea air wafts by, and I take a deep breath. We drive onto what might be a ferry or barge, from noises I hear.

My eyes fly open. They must be taking me to Cedar Island and admitting me to Shore Lodge, like I heard Mom mention. I'll be behind locked doors in a secure ward on an isolated island. I try to scream, but words don't come out. A monitor beeps faster.

A man in a blue uniform says in a stern voice, "Settle down, or I'll have to give you a sedative."

I thrash and kick, legs lashing out. My heart races, and my armpits are damp. A machine beeps with more intensity. What fresh hell have I entered?

The attendant reaches over, doing something to an IV in my arm. A rush of calm enters my bloodstream, and my muscles relax. The monitor's beeping slows down.

With a gentle bump, I'm guessing the ferry landed on the Cedar Island side of the channel. The vehicle we're in drives off. We turn onto a gravel road, and the ambulance slows.

I don't want to be in this body, entombed in silence. If I could just go back in time.

Attendants roll me out of the van and into a building, going down a hall to an elevator, where we go up one floor. Exiting the elevator on the second floor, the lemon-scented air gives me a bitter taste in my mouth.

"Transfer for you," a man says.

I hear a woman screeching and shrieking, giving me a headache. She mumbles and sings about a cheating husband.

A woman I seem to recognize signs paperwork and says, "Let's transfer this new patient to a wheelchair."

Workers in white shift my body, moving me to the chair. They strap me in around the waist. My head feels heavy. I blink at the stark walls and harsh florescent lights.

The nurse says in a commanding voice, "Have a good trip back."

The ambulance attendants march away with lighter footsteps, rolling a gurney.

The nurse puts her hands on her hips. "Well, Dusty Stone, my word. I never would have predicted I'd see you here as a resident. But life has little surprises, doesn't it? Don't worry, we'll make you comfortable."

I try to groan but can't make a sound.

She pats my arm. "You look scared, and it is scary at first to be here. Your mother didn't understand that or adjust, but I hope you'll do better than she did and accept where you are, making the most of it."

Thank you for reading *Avalanche*! Please let other readers know what to expect by posting ratings and reviews on Goodreads, Amazon and BookBub.

Next up is Book 4, *These Lies*, in the *Jacklyn Stone Thriller Series.*

Sign up on my website www.susanspechtoram.com for my author newsletter to hear about new releases and bookish news.

Follow me on BookBub for updates: https://www. bookbub.com/authors/susan-specht-oram

My Facebook author page is Susan Specht Oram Author

My YouTube channel @susanspechtoramauthor features nature photography and author chats.

Thank you for reading my books!

ABOUT THE AUTHOR

Susan is writing mysteries-thrillers and creative nonfiction. Previously, she served as senior director of corporate communications for biotechnology companies. Susan worked as an activity aide in an upscale nursing home's secure psychiatric unit. She was a potter and painter with an art studio in Seattle and has also worked as a market researcher, a nurse's aide, a waitress, and a library page. Her essays have been published in Mothering Magazine, Twins Magazine and Utne Reader.

Susan grew up near Detroit, Michigan and received a BFA with Honors from University of Oregon and a MBA from Seattle University. She lives in a windy part of the Pacific Northwest with her husband and rescue dog.

Novels by Susan Specht Oram
  Shore Lodge
  The Thieves
  Cabin Eight
  Secrets at the Café
  The Mother's Threat

Under Jackson Bridge

Missing Man

By Midnight

The Winter Storm

The Cold Night

Avalanche

These Lies (coming December 2025)

Creative nonfiction: Strangers on a Train Series

Green Light

The Train

Canoe

Soup Kettle

Bathtub

Phone Call

Watering Can

Waterfall

Strangers on a Train series collection (Books 1-8)

Humorous fiction:

Boating with Buddy, a report from a canine correspondent

Nonfiction:

Brief business books on investor relations, crisis communication and public relations

www.ingramcontent.com/pod-product-compliance
Lightning Source LLC
Chambersburg PA
CBHW071600110726
47908CB00007B/2175